If you want to read a book which has been soaked in fasting, prayer, and tears, then you've selected the right author. Debbie's experiences in the upbringing of eight children, who are all living for the Lord, will inspire, mentor, and serve as an enriching resource for you.

> —*Dr. Adonna Otwell*
> *Chair, Department of General Studies*
> *Southwestern Assemblies of God*
> *University*

Debbie Bridgewater is a multi-talented woman of God, Pastor's wife, and a mom on a mission. She has competently achieved with ease a functional, organized, secure, and God-filled home environment for her wonderful family. In today's busy lifestyle she goes about her tasks as someone dedicated to the call of God on her life, making time for the important and the mundane; the serious and the humorous. She's learned that people are always more important than things and finds creative ways to schedule her workload around those dearest to her heart: God and her loving family. In essence we know Debbie to be a Proverbs 31 woman. We are blessed to call her friend and we heartily endorse this tremendous book. Not only will you learn valuable lessons to share with others, you'll also discover the timeless treasure of a life dedicated to fulfill God's call and destiny for your life. This book will leave you encouraged, refreshed and mobilized for whatever tasks today may require of you.

> —*Dr. Rudi and Sharon Swanepoel*
> *God's Glory Ministries International*

A woman of integrity, wisdom, sensitivity, and leadership is the best way to describe Debbie Bridgewater. Being a pastor's wife would be challenging enough to keep life in order, but she's also a mother of 8 precious and talented children. Her servant's heart and kind and gentle spirit are proof that God has given her special gifts. From her scrumptious cooking to her beautiful and peaceful home and family, if Debbie has something to say, we're listening!

—*Greg & Glenda Bostock*
Blastoff Ministries

I have met few people in my life who are as beautifully genuine as Debbie Bridgewater. She is one of those true treasures, an individual always aglow with the presence of Jesus. I have worked with her in ministry situations for many years and have marveled at her Godly wisdom and loving heart. I am also privileged to call Debbie my friend and have so appreciated how she manages Marriage, Ministry, and Motherhood with such grace and creativity. Truly, if there is a real "superwoman" I believe her name is Debbie!

—*Lisa Marie Buster*
Lisa Marie Buster Ministries

Domestic Diva

The Lost Art of Homemaking

Be a "Diva!"
Debbie Bridgewater
Ps. 90:17

Debbie Bridgewater

Domestic Diva
Copyright © 2010 by Debbie Bridgewater

Unless otherwise noted, Scripture taken from the New King James Version. Copyright © 1982 by Thomas Nelson, Inc. Used by permission. All rights reserved.

Borderline Publishing LLC
305 N. Steelhead Way
Boise, ID 83704
www.borderlinepublishing.com

ISBN 978-0984504558 (Paperback)

Cover design by Julia Lukomsky

Printed in the United States of America on post-consumer recycled paper

Acknowledgments

Thanks to my family and many friends who encouraged me to write this book; to my prayer partners, Adonna Otwell and Christy Mercer, who faithfully prayed me through long months of writing; to my editors Gwin Spencer, Amber Bridgewater, Kayla Morton, and Janae Stockham who helped refine my writing; to Sharon Swanepoel, speaker and author of children's books, who encouraged me along the way to keep writing because "God has a plan"; to Gwin Spencer who never let me forget God had a great plan for my life, encouraging me to write this book for the many young women she ministers to and counsels with; to my cover designer, Julia Lukomsky and graphic artist, Ty Pauls who worked furiously yet patiently to meet my deadlines; to my son Isaac who at 14 years of age, asked me to write a recipe book, "just in case he marries someone who can't cook!" Way to plan ahead Isaac! To my husband Tim who has always believed in me, seeing in me what I couldn't see in myself; and last but definitely not least, my Lord and Savior, Jesus Christ, who called me to a ministry much bigger than myself...writing this book. God, you amaze me daily at what you can do through an obedient servant! I LOVE YOU WITH MY WHOLE HEART, SOUL, MIND, AND STRENGTH!

Dedication

I dedicate this book to my family: All eight children...Benjamin, Jesse, Josiah, Briana, Isaac, Andrew, Aaron, and Christopher, who walks with me patiently and unconditionally in love through many changes and seasons of life, good and bad; and especially to my loving Pastor and husband Tim, who saw me as *'A diamond in the rough'* when we started dating. We are preparing to celebrate 28 wonderful years of laughter, challenges, heartache, and personal growth in marriage, changing us into the servants of God we are today! I love you Tim and my children; you are truly God's gift to me!

AUTHOR'S NOTE

MY SACRED RESPONSIBILITY and PRIVILEGE

Writing a book was something this girl never dreamed she would do. After all, I am an average wife, mother, and homemaker with only one difference—I have an above average number of children, eight to be exact. I am grateful for the turning of the tide and a greater acceptance of large families in our day.

When asked how I do what I do, my response is that our wonderful Savior equips us with all we need to fulfill the work He has for us. A friend told me once many years ago, "God gives us one more child than we think we can handle; that way, we give up and He takes over!" One day another friend called me "Wonder Woman"; my response? "The only wonder in this woman is that there's any sanity left in me at the end of the day!" With so many thoughts, questions, and misconceptions about what I do as a homemaker and how I do it, I feel a mandate from God to write down the wisdom, knowledge, and experience I have gained—all because of Him.

My dream and goal in writing this book is to encourage you in the awesome call to be a help meet, mother, and homemaker, equipping women to pursue this wonderful life of ministry to their families. If I accomplish this, I will be greatly satisfied that God has worked through me as I serve Him in this sacred responsibility and calling!

"And let the beauty of the Lord our God be upon us, and establish the work of our hands for us; yes, establish the work of our hands." (Psalm 90:17)

—Debbie L. Bridgewater,
Licensed Minister with the Assemblies of God
Fellowship

FORWARD

I remember the first time I came to the Bridgewater house. I knocked on the door and two cute, little, towhead-blonde boys answered. I was invited in and introduced to Tim and Debbie by their son, whom I was friends with. I distinctly remember the genuine smile I was given by Debbie, which said to me, "Welcome to our home, we're so glad to meet you and have you here," without actually uttering any words to me. I felt welcomed in a big way. It's no wonder that I kept coming back!

It's important to understand that I wasn't in a situation of coming from an unstable home. I wasn't looking for love or affection from a mom or a dad or to have the feel of a family. I was given that in surplus by my own wonderful, loving parents. But I did begin to grow in a relationship with Tim and Debbie and the rest of their family. I started to come over more often (Sometimes purposely around dinner time because I just couldn't get enough of those cheesy potatoes!), and I quickly saw how the Bridgewater house was run and how they functioned together as a family.

I have seen firsthand the love and affection that Tim and Debbie have for their children, as well as their ability to lovingly discipline them. They truly exemplify the way in which God's love is portrayed for all in 1 John 4:19 that "we love each other because He loved us first" (NLT). Tim and Debbie loved and respected their children first and, as a result, gained their children's love and respect back.

I have always been intrigued by the "Proverbs 31 woman" and hope to someday exemplify that for my own husband and family. So, naturally, I was excited to hear that Debbie was writing a book on this subject. This book will show you how to become the woman that God intended you to be for not only your husband and your family, but also those around you, those you minister to and encounter on a daily basis. It is my personal opinion that Debbie epitomizes the "Proverbs 31 woman." Though she isn't perfect, she is a great representative of God's vision for a woman whether a working woman or stay at home mom (and in my opinion Debbie is both of these). Her personal walk with God is evident in her daily life, and she portrays it through everything from doing the dishes to preaching! Debbie understands that her life doesn't revolve around her, but instead, her purpose is to serve those around her. She does everything for the work of His kingdom, not for the promotion of herself. There are times when I think she must have some sort of super-human qualities to be able to function on so little sleep or to be able to prepare food for hundreds of people at once or to just keep up with the chaos that can be the routine of life. But she has shown me that it is through self-discipline, determination, love, and the grace and strength of God that she has been able to do all she does.

I trust that through reading this book you will be encouraged to become a "Domestic Diva", exemplifying the Proverbs 31 woman in today's world. This book is full of godly wisdom and practical examples of things that have proven themselves to work. I hope that whether you are in college and unmarried like me, or married to the love of your life, you find an abundance of joy and knowledge reading this book, as I know I did.

—Chrissie Hepworth,
Pre-Med Student, Northwest University

Contents

Introduction

At 14 years of age, I met the man who would eventually become my husband. We were the same age and, within two years of first meeting, began dating at 16. Tim's Dad holds the honor for setting us up. He called my mother, talked for a few minutes, then proceeded to scheme a way to get us talking over the phone. We both got on the line and following a 20 minute chat, a date was planned for that evening. This was just the beginning of our relationship, and at the young age of 18, we were married. We have had the average struggles as well as many great times together. I understand now that it wasn't just my father-in-law that set us up; he was just the tool God used to put a relationship together that would stand the test of time on the Solid Rock!

Our first baby came along nearly five years into the marriage; a long, difficult labor caused me to think he would be an only child. As God in all His wisdom would have it, the thrill of a precious new baby would cause me to forget the pain, and two years later, I delivered another baby boy one month early. As a child, I had planned to have only two children, but loving motherhood so much, I longed for more babies. After delivering our third son, my husband was done, feeling our family complete. Emotionally I struggled with wanting more babies. I began praying for God to take away this desire from me or change my husband's heart. I would soon find out baby number four was on her way. God had changed Tim's heart and told him we would have a girl.

Although we thought that our family was complete, I discovered we would indeed have another baby. Four months into the pregnancy, I began having complications. God's grace and mercy were abundant, and He spared baby number five. Although I suffered complications following delivery, God was with me, and we had five healthy children.

Eventually, our family would grow to eight children ... seven boys and one girl. I totally connected to the old television show of "Eight is Enough!" I was done! Three years following the birth of my last baby, I discovered baby number nine was on the way. What a surprise, thinking my days of fertility were over. Unfortunately, this beautiful, tiny life inside me wouldn't survive, and I miscarried at five weeks gestation.

From that heartache, God gave Tim and me a message of "Undervalued Blessings." This became a turning point in my life, a time of searching and seeking God deeper than ever before. I came to realize we tend to overlook blessings and become unable to see things for what they really are: God working in our lives and giving us blessings in disguise. My husband and eight children were my greatest blessings and focus in ministry, but life as I knew it was getting ready to change. God would use ALL my experiences for His glory and prepare me for ministry I never dreamed possible.

About eight years ago, God began calling me to a greater level of ministry and commitment; writing a book was part of that call. My first response to God was, "There is NO way I can do that!" I am a mother of eight, football mom, and home educator with never-ending laundry, cleaning, and cooking at home. On top of that, I am a Pastor's wife and Bible Study teacher. How can I possibly fit anything else into my schedule? I finally gave in to God, remembering that if He calls, He also equips us with everything we need to fulfill His call.

I never once thought what I do to be unusual—caring for a busy household; operating on a tight budget; teaching, training, and preparing my children for adulthood; organizing busy schedules; operating in my role as a pastor's wife; teaching Bible Study—all things I've done for so long they are second nature. When young ladies began coming to me for counsel and help, I was shocked. Things which seemed obvious to me were not obvious to others. I have come to realize the current generation is growing up in such a busy, rushed, two-income society that little training is happening in the home. This isn't to condemn anyone; it simply states the fact of how our culture and society has changed, and the training which used to happen in every home, happens in very few today. In the 1800s, by the time children were 12 years old, girls were taught to run the household and boys the farm. Children today are graduating from high school with little direction in life, and neither girls nor boys know much about what it takes to run a home on a budget in today's economy.

More and more often, ladies began contacting me asking for advice about how to cook, how to train their children, and simply how I do what I do. At the same time, many others were asking me to write a book. This was all confirmation for the call I knew God had placed on my life. Last year during a time of personal prayer, I felt God heavily impress on my heart, "It's time!" I knew exactly what God was saying: it was time to start the book. What an honor God has given me to share with you my experiences, wisdom, and knowledge, all which He gave to me. I know God has a call to ministry for everyone and I believe that call starts in the home. This is God's work, not mine. As you read through these pages, do it prayerfully allowing God to speak to you and create a greater longing in your heart to **be the very best "Domestic Diva" you can be.**

Part One

Domestic Diva's Roles in the Home

The Proverbs 31 Diva

Reading Proverbs 31 can be overwhelming to even the most efficient woman. I mean really, who can possibly do all these things? It appears she was perfect in every way. Never a ho-hum day or a harsh word crossed her path. She had everything ready on time or early; she sewed, cleaned, cooked, canned, and cared for her husband and children who only blessed her; her fire never went out by night, and she got up early while it was still dark outside. She even had a business! Didn't she ever sleep? Doesn't it seem unfair that to a Christian, this perfect woman would be God's model for us?

First of all, you can rest in the fact that the Proverbs 31 woman was not a real person. She is descriptive of a perfect model for young men to pursue in looking for the ideal wife. This virtuous woman demonstrates for us every area of being a godly wife and homemaker, showing how we can fulfill our God-given responsibilities with dignity. She excelled in her role as the ultimate Domestic Diva, glamorous and successful in caring for the affairs of the home, the most excellent example for all generations past, present, and still to come.

If you notice, Proverbs 31 never mentions her physical attributes. King Lemuel's mother was a very wise woman, one who understood completely her own words in verse 30, **"Favor is deceitful, and beauty is vain (*useless*);**

but a woman that fears the Lord, she shall be praised." Ladies, your worth goes way beyond any physical attributes you have. It has everything to do with your fear of God, and out of that fear flows respect, love, and selfless service to your family.

The word virtuous is described in Webster's Dictionary as: "Pure, modest, decent; pure in thought and action; refrain from sexual immorality (*sexually pure*)." Let's look briefly at Proverbs 31:10-31, verse by verse to see what made the Proverbs 31 Diva a model for us to live by.

Verse 10: "Who can find a virtuous wife? For her price is far above rubies." There is not enough wealth in the world to purchase the beauty in godly character and contentment that comes with a virtuous woman/wife. She is priceless!

Verse 11: "The heart of her husband safely trusts in her, so that he will have no lack of gain." He has no need to worry that she might do something to damage his reputation. He trusts that while he is providing for his family, she is taking care of the day-to- day affairs of the household. She won't spend money frivolously, so her husband and family can prosper.

Verse 12: "She does him good and not evil all the days of her life." She will do everything possible to pursue good for her husband, always speaking well of him. He is a gift from God. She loves him and no evil is ever devised toward him. She will not manipulate situations to get her own way but will seek to prefer his desires over her own.

Verse 13: "She seeks wool and flax, and willingly works with her hands." Our Proverbs 31 Diva provides clothing for her family, looking for the most economical way to purchase them. (Although you may not sew, you can shop sales, clearance, and second-hand stores to find the best possible prices to clothe your family.) The idea is to purchase the best possible product for the best possible price.

Verse 14: "She is like the merchant ships, she brings her food from afar." The implication here suggests that the Proverbs 31 Diva is willing to go where needed to purchase the best food for the best prices, finding availability and going the extra mile for her family. She likely preserved food in season to provide during off-season or winter months when fruits and vegetables were no longer available.

Verse 15: "She also rises while it is yet night and provides food for her household and a portion for her maidservants." A virtuous woman is productive and definitely not lazy. She gets up early in the morning to plan for the day's meals, making certain all members of her household are well taken care of. She is self-disciplined, pushing herself from bed when she'd prefer to sleep in, arising to plan the daily meals and begin the preparation process to ensure her family and household members have everything they need for the day's activities.

Verse 16: "She considers a field, and buys it; from her profits, she plants a vineyard." Industrious is the proper adjective here. She is not afraid of hard work but looks for every means possible to contribute to the family income and resources. There is no substitute for hard work! She plants a seed and reaps a harvest!

Verse 17: "She girds herself with strength and strengthens her arms." She prepares for work by adorning herself with proper work attire, wearing clothes conducive to hard work outside and inside her home, putting on necessary wraps and girdles to strengthen her body and arms for heavier work. There was no fear of *breaking a nail*, and her hard work brought about great rewards!

Verse 18: "She perceives that her merchandise is good and her lamp does not go out by night." She does a job well and to completion, one to be proud of. In her culture, a candle was kept lit in the window to welcome strangers that might need a room to retire in for the night. She was always ready and prepared to host someone who might need a place to stay or get in out of the cold. A hospitable and welcoming spirit was part of her character. She extended hospitality to all!

Verse 19: "She stretches out her hands to the distaff and her hand holds the spindle." Again, the Virtuous Woman is using her resources to provide very necessary items for running a household. In this scripture, she spins thread, making use of the flax she likely grew herself to make clothes and other garments. She models an energetic and diligent spirit.

Verse 20: "She extends her hand to the poor; yes, she reaches out her hands to the needy." God's Word is very clear on the blessings and benefits that come from helping the poor and needy. The Proverbs 31 woman understood that this was part of the character of a godly woman, helping those less fortunate with what God has blessed her with.

Verse 21: "She is not afraid of snow for her household, for all her household is clothed with scarlet." Scarlet represents warmth and prosperity. Her family stayed warm and dressed in style. She spent a fraction of the money that it takes to purchase clothing at the market because she sewed their garments, acquiring necessities in the most economical way.

Verse 22: "She makes tapestry for herself; her clothing is fine linen and purple." Again, she wore classy garments. Diligence in hard work gave her the ability to clothe herself in style and class. She was frugal with the finances yet looked like a *million bucks*!

Verse 23: "Her husband is known in the gates when he sits among the elders of the land." It's amazing what a good reputation does! The Proverbs 31 Diva has within her the ability to build up her husband, causing him to be well-known and respected in the community. Because of her integrity, she builds him up among peers, enhancing his great reputation.

Verse 24: "She makes linen garments and sells them; and supplies sashes for the merchants." She is a woman who knows how to make extra money, helping with the home finances. Her talents and abilities have provided a means to create and sell items, bringing needed money into her family's economy.

Verse 25: "Strength and honor are her clothing; she shall rejoice in time to come." Inner strength exhibits character and integrity, bringing honor and favor from God and others. She wears it well and will rejoice in the time to come because she daily lays the groundwork of good home management and genuine love for her family.

Verse 26: "She opens her mouth with wisdom; and on her tongue is the law of kindness." This is a woman that speaks wisdom and possesses the fruit of the Spirit. She is full of God, the source from which all wisdom comes, and she exhibits well the fruit of the Spirit—love, joy, peace, patience, gentleness, goodness, faith, meekness, and temperance—always preferring others.

Verse 27: "She watches over the ways of her household, and does not eat the bread of idleness."

She is too busy caring for her home to allow for any idleness. She hasn't the time for idle talk or gossip, anything that wastes time and lacks productivity. She utilizes her time and resources well in looking after every aspect of her household.

Verse 28: "Her children rise up and call her blessed; her husband also and he praises her." She successfully models a godly wife and mother, so now her family praises her. They are grateful for the excellent Diva she is and now give her verbal accolades for all to hear. Has she been perfect? No, of course not, but she lives with an upright heart, modeling character and integrity in all she does.

Verse 29: "Many daughters have done well, but you excel them all." There are many powerful, righteous, chaste, efficacious, and morally excellent women, but she excelled them all. Her heart was perfectly in tune with the heart of God, giving her the edge over all other women, something she aspired to and has now achieved.

Verse 30: "Charm is deceitful and beauty is vain, but a woman who fears the Lord, she shall be praised." Many women know the art of charming momentarily with their beauty, but she is a woman with an authentic fear of and respect for God; she will be rightly praised for years to come.

Verse 31: "Give her of the fruit of her hands; and let her own works praise her in the gates." Her works and genuine heart speak for themselves. No one need comment or tell her story; actions truly speak louder than words! She doesn't just talk the talk, she walks the walk!

The conclusion of this entire passage is fear of the Lord, an understanding of who God is and who He created us to be. If we will operate in our high calling of wife and mother in accordance with God's Word, then we can excel in that calling and be successful Proverbs 31 *Domestic Divas* in the 21st Century!

Tag from Tim, a husband's perspective:

I am sure I have said it at least a thousand times; I simply don't understand how she does it all! Not only is she a model Proverbs 31 Diva, she is also a woman of deep prayer. I truly consider myself to be one of the most blessed men on the planet, for God has given me a fabulous woman who is kind and considerate, an incredibly hard worker, a wonderful cook, a caring mother, and the icing on the cake is that after all these years of marriage and 8 children later, she continues to be very attractive, having maintained her youthful figure. Above all, I am blessed to have a wife who loves God with all her heart, soul, mind, and strength. I suspect He enables her to love me as much as she does.

Coming from a man's perspective, I cannot think of any Christian male who wouldn't love to have a woman who applies the principals contained herein. Even now I am remembering all the accolades I received recently from a group of men I took on what we call "Encounter." Debbie had prepared all the food from scratch for these men and sent it with me. Needless to say, the men raved over the food, even asking for recipes to share with their wives. So go ahead get started, you won't be disappointed.

Intentionally Created

Have you ever felt like an after-thought? Like maybe you were just overlooked the first time? Reading Genesis chapter 2, verse 7, we see God created man and then proceeded to give him dominion over the earth. Eleven verses later, God says, **"It isn't good for man to be alone."** What took Him so long to decide He needed to create a woman? Did it take God eleven verses to realize man couldn't do it on his own, so He needed to *create* man a helper?

At times while reading scripture I think about these things. In all reality, I know God had a plan before creation, and that plan included the relationships between men and women; we weren't an after-thought at all. We were in God's original plan, a plan which included a beautiful coming together of a man and a woman to procreate and see families birthed into God's creation. God knew all along that a man would need a woman in order to see creation come into perfect fullness. Isn't it interesting that a woman would be created from a rib, out of the side of a man? She would be created to come along side and complete him.

Genesis 2:18 tells us that God created woman as a *help meet* to man. A *help meet* is what we were *intentionally* created to be, definitely not an afterthought or because the original plan didn't work. **Psalm 139** says we were "fearfully and wonderfully made; fashioned when there was as yet none of us." Jeremiah 29:11 says "He gives us an *expected end*." In other words, He planned our lives before we were ever fashioned in the womb. What a beautiful thought that God knew us and planned us before He created all things!

Although created in the image of God, some women have decided that the beauty of being a *help meet* to a man was not for them. Unfortunately because of this these women miss out on one of the greatest blessings life has to offer: a perfect union and relationship with her husband, including ministry to her family. May this chapter stir up the gift in you to minister exactly as God planned for your life, as a *help meet* to your husband!

So what is a *help meet*? A help meet is a helper that is well suited to meet someone's needs; in the home, it means we were created to help our husbands by meeting *his* needs. **Proverbs 18:22 says, "He who finds a wife finds a good thing!"** We *are* a good thing! **Proverbs 19:14** says, **"A prudent wife is from the Lord."** A prudent wife is one that shows good judgment, discretion, and frugality. She will be modest in thought, action, and dress. If this is the type of woman that comes from the Lord, then we can safely say that any action which is contrary to prudence would not be of the Lord. If God gives us to our husbands to be *help meets*, then we must be prudent to be considered a *good thing* as a *help meet*.

I remember sitting with a group of ministers discussing the infamous "Wardrobe Malfunction" incident with Janet Jackson at the half time show during the 38th Super Bowl in 2004. I commented how glad I was that my family wasn't watching the Super Bowl and how uncomfortable it must have been for wives watching with their husbands. One of the pastors piped up saying he wasn't bothered by the incident because he wasn't a *prude*. I was somewhat shocked due to the fact prudence is still a quality for virtue.

My husband does a lot of pre-marital counseling with couples and every time he begins to speak of the roles each partner is to assume in the home, the girls bristle. They don't want to submit to anyone, including their soon-to-be husband. These women see this as a weakness; like they are somehow second rate. God doesn't create anything second rate, only first class! By submitting to your husband you are, in essence, submitting to God and His plan for your life. As Tim continues to explain how wonderful a relationship can be when both the husband and wife agree to the biblical, God-ordained order in the home, the wife-to-be relaxes and realizes that it can and will work when both are on board with God's plan.

It's easy to submit to a husband who treats his wife like Christ treats the church. The very nature of submission, however, comes when you have to give yourself over to a final decision that you don't necessarily agree with. To give you an example, if your husband came home from work and said to you, "Honey, we are being transferred to Hawaii," and you've always wanted to live in Hawaii, you would agree and jump fully on board with his decision. This is NOT submission. However, if he came home and said, "Honey, we are moving to Barrow, Alaska, the most northern point in North America that stays below freezing even most of the summer," and you hate the cold, this would be a very difficult decision to jump on board with. If after much discussion, your husband still feels like this is the only option for work, it would take true submission on your part to say, "Okay, I'll follow you."

God, in all His wisdom, made man to be the leader in the home to establish order. Two people with authority to make a final decision will eventually clash, creating a volatile situation and problems in the relationship. A true *help meet* will help her husband by supporting his decisions even when she doesn't agree. I assure you, if this is God's plan, He will bless you for living out the role of a helper and walking in submission to your husband. This is not to say women have no part in the decision-making process, quite the contrary. If you have proven trustworthiness as a *help meet*, your husband will listen to you and value all your input, having confidence in your sound advice and godly wisdom.

A great marriage is one which both husband and wife operate in their roles, allowing the other to complete him/her. Men are to be assertive (not dictating), while a wise woman will allow her husband to be the leader and complement him with her femininity. Oh, the power of a woman that is feminine and supportive to her husband, loving him even when he makes mistakes. She will be a *help meet*, helping him walk through failures or disappointments and making him think he's the most amazing man in the world! She will love him, fulfilling his physical and emotional needs. A man will melt before a woman that builds him up; conversely, he will become an angry, frustrated man when married to a woman that tears him down. **Proverbs 14:1** says, **"Every wise woman builds her house, but the foolish woman pulls it down with her hands."** As women, it is within our power to have a peaceful, godly, and stable home, where our husbands love to share life with us. The home reflects the attitude and heart of the wife.

I have learned to be thankful to God for my husband, seeing him as one of God's greatest gifts to me. Is he perfect? No, but he is a godly man who treats me with honor and dignity, serving God with his whole life. I started the habit of thinking about and thanking God for

Tim's good qualities every morning when I wake up, every night when I lay down in bed, *and* every time he irritates me. It is very difficult to remain upset with someone when you are considering all their good qualities, refusing to dwell on the bad. Let's face it, we all have irritating habits that, if dwelt on every day, would not only damage but ultimately destroy a relationship.

While teaching a ladies' Bible study one evening, I asked all the women to join me in this exercise of thinking on the positive things about their husbands and giving encouraging words to him. One lady requested prayer due to the fact that her husband was verbally abusive to her. I prayed for and reminded her of the homework assignment: build up your husband with words of affirmations and encouragement, even if it's difficult at best some days. The following week she returned with the report that after speaking to him of her feelings and hurts when he talks to her that way, he listened and hadn't spoke another negative word to her since. That's the power of prayer and the power of kind words in a relationship.

Romans 12:9-18 exhorts us to love as a Christian should:

> **"Let love be without hypocrisy.**
> **Abhor what is evil.**
> **Cling to what is good.**
> **Be kindly affectionate to one another with**
> **brotherly love, in honor giving preference to**
> **one another.**
> **Not lagging in diligence.**
> **Fervent in spirit.**
> **Serving the Lord.**
> **Rejoicing in hope.**
> **Patient in tribulation, continuing steadfastly in**
> **prayer.**

Distributing to the needs of the saints.
Given to hospitality.
Bless those who persecute you; bless and do not
  curse.
Rejoice with those who rejoice, and weep with
  those who weep.
Be of the same mind toward one another.
Do not set your mind on high things, but associate
  with the humble.
Do not be wise in your own opinion.
Repay no one evil for evil.
Have regard for good things in the sight of all
  men.
If it is possible, as much as depends on you, live
  peaceably with all men.
Beloved, do not avenge yourselves, but rather give
  place to wrath; for it is written, vengeance is
  Mine, I will repay says the Lord.
Therefore if your enemy hungers, feed him; if he
  thirst, give him a drink; for in doing so you will
  heap coals of fire on his head.
Do not be overcome with evil but overcome evil
  with good."

Imagine what kind of an amazing relationships could be fostered if we would live by this one passage of scripture; if we showed authentic love through kindness, honor, preferring one another, praying for each other, exhibiting patience, rejoicing and weeping together, not pressing our opinion but hearing theirs, and serving each other with all humility. As mentioned in verse 18, "**Live peaceably with ALL people, as much as depends on you.**" We have the responsibility to get along with others! By living according to Romans, we can love unconditionally, treating our husbands with all the respect and honor they deserve as leaders in our homes. When this type of relationship is cultivated, it's easy to submit and be an amazing *help meet* to our husband!

I want to share with you some practical ways we can be a wonderful *help meet*. Before going into fulltime ministry, Tim worked as a District Manager for a food service corporation that operated business and college dining accounts. He traveled on a regular basis and worked long hours. We were accustomed to him working 12-14 hour days, 5-6 days a week and some weeks he worked all 7 days. Due to Tim being exceptionally tired when he got off work in the evening, I always made an effort to have our home tidied up, dinner cooking, and kids orderly before he walked through the door.

Most of you are likely *not* in that position; however, no matter the number of hours your husband works, he wants to come home to you and his children in a peaceful home atmosphere. Most husbands don't like chaos. If you are a stay at home mom, you have the pleasure of setting the atmosphere and tone of your home all day. You've heard the saying, *"If momma ain't happy, ain't nobody happy!" If you ain't happy momma, then do something about it 'cause your husband ain't happy if you ain't happy!* Find out what your husband likes when he walks in the door from work, and try to accommodate him. Some like downtime, while others like lots of attention from the kids. Know what he likes, and then work to meet his needs. Soft worship or instrumental music sets a peaceful, relaxed atmosphere in the home. If you happen to have overly energetic children, good music can settle them, creating a peaceful environment when their daddy gets home from work.

To encourage more family time together in the evening, I might suggest that you take care of the day-to-day responsibilities, as much as you can do, to free up time for

your husband. Some of you have never touched a lawn
mower, much less mowed a lawn. This would be a great
time to learn. Years ago my oldest son Ben was presented
with the opportunity to work in Alaska for the summer,
helping to build a hanger and duplex on an airstrip with a
pilot friend of ours. This opportunity was too good for
Ben to pass up. He was working on his pilot's license and
would get to do some flying after work if he took the job. I
decided that our son Jesse and I would take over Ben's
lawn service, so he would be free to go. This meant I had
to learn to use all the equipment plus back up a trailer,
something I had never done before. You really can teach
an old dog new tricks; I proved it! We survived the
summer, and I found there were things I could do if I just
challenged myself. There are so many tasks around the
home that we can learn to do which would take a big load
of responsibility off our husbands and free them up to
spend extra time with us.

Cleaning our garage is one thing I really dislike, but my
husband greatly appreciates when I do it. Some projects
aren't fun, but did anyone say that every job is fun? Look
for things your husband would normally do when off work
and see if it's something you could accomplish for him;
then put on grungy clothes, roll up your sleeves, and get
busy! You will not only impress yourself, but you will also
impress the man you married when you remove tasks from
the honey-do list.

I want to end this chapter with an admonition to you
concerning modesty and discretion. You were perfectly
suited to be *your* husband's *help meet*, no one else's. You
honor your husband by being modest and discrete in the
way you dress and present yourself. Tell your man by the
clothes you wear that you are saving everything for him
and offering it to no one else. Cover yourself so as not to
cause any other man to lust or stumble in his thoughts.

Keep yourself ONLY for the man you married and no one else through the way you dress. Your husband will appreciate and honor you for this, and you will once again fulfill your role as the perfect *help meet* and match for him: a beautiful, ***Intentionally Created***, **Proverbs 31, Domestic Diva!**

Tag from Tim, a husband's perspective:

I can't think of one Christian who believes the Holy Spirit got a raw deal when He came to walk along side us, to help us all be what we cannot be on our own. A close study will reveal the similarities between the role of a woman and the role of the Holy Spirit. So go ahead and fulfill your God-given role of being the best help meet on the planet.

Submission is more than obedience. We can all obey yet inwardly grumble. Submission is surrendering your will to the other. In other words, submission is not submission until you do what you don't want to do. Submission in the context of the marriage is placing your heart and life in the hands of your husband. Your husband on the other hand will be greatly influenced by your desires. In fact, whenever possible, he will place your desires ahead of his own. The husband's position is to give his life for his wife and family, typically placing his own desires behind those of his family. The model is really the husband and the wife giving to each other with a heart of love.

Gift of Hospitality

Visiting my friend Anita's home is like going to the best five-star restaurant in town. She is Filipino, and her cooking is a wonderful mix of Ethnic and American foods with her trademark: lumpia and scalloped pineapple. Mmmmmm, I can taste it now. The multiple meats, salads, and rice are just the beginning. Then, she brings out her display of desserts, and, oh my, I'm so full but can't help myself; I have to indulge just a little longer. I'm always completely stuffed when I leave—someone just roll me out to the car please!

Anita's home is modest, neat, tidy, and beautifully decorated. For guests fortunate enough to spend the night there, the accommodations are found to be impeccable! I call Anita the "Queen of Hospitality." This is truly her gift; she does it well and with as much grace as anyone I know. I feel like a privileged guest every time I enter her home, even though I've known her for many years.

I can remember when I first started dating my husband. I would go to his home, and his mother always had more than enough food for whoever happened to be there. Many times friends and family would pop in unannounced at dinner, and she would tell them to pull up a chair and have something to eat. Her home was always well kept, maintained, clean, and decorated. When Tim and I decided to get married, I felt intimidated by my mother-in-law-to-be and concerned how I would ever be able to prepare those meals and keep a home like she did. My own mother taught me many things, such as how to clean, cook, garden, and can but with a simplified approach. Meals were meat, potatoes, and vegetables, while home furnishings were the bare necessities. Mom was great with keeping a home simplified and getting rid of things that weren't necessary. Rarely, was there ever clutter around the house, and it was always clean and sanitized. I can learn much from both of them.

Knowing that I would have a husband to please who was accustomed to different types of meals and collectable furnishings frightened me a little. His mother cooked his favorite meals from memory, without using recipes. How could I possibly learn to prepare these items without *instructions*? How could I ever have people drop in and be confident enough to have them stay for dinner, much less have my house spotless all the time just in case someone did drop by? These were very real questions and great concerns from a soon-to-be bride.

Maybe you have had these same concerns either in the past or are facing them now. Let me set your mind at ease. You don't have to be like your mother, your mother-in-law, or anyone else you know that may be greatly gifted in the area of hospitality. God made each of us with our own unique gifts, and we need not try to copy someone else's. However, just because we may not think we have the *gift of hospitality*, doesn't negate our God-given responsibility to be hospitable.

In speaking of loving others, behaving like a Christian, living right, and serving others for God's glory, both Peter and Paul exhort us to be hospitable. **Romans 12:13, "... distributing to the needs of the saints, given to**

hospitality." And **I Peter 4:9-10, "Be hospitable one to
another without grumbling. As each one has received
a gift, minister it to one another, as good stewards of
the manifold grace of God."** In other words, we all have
been given a gift to minister hospitality to one another as
"good stewards of God's grace and love."

Keep in mind that you don't have to serve a five-course
meal or have a perfectly spotless home. No fine china or
extravagant table and glassware are needed to invite
people into your home. Never feel intimidated that you
can't cook as well as someone else or have a fancy home
and extravagant furnishings like others you know. You
simply need a heart that says, "I love you and want to
serve you," according to God's Word.

In my many years of practicing hospitality, I have found
that most people don't remember what they ate or even
how it tasted. They don't usually keep account of how
intricately you cleaned your home or whether you served a
meal on paper plates or fine china. They remember you
taking time to show them love by inviting them into your
home and serving them. They remember the gracious
fellowship, the hot beverage on a cold day and a cool glass
of water on a hot day. They'll remember the game you
played or the way you paid attention to the conversation
with them. People have a deep need for relationships
which are met by fellowshipping with one another.

If this is new territory to you, remember the only way to
get comfortable with hospitality is to just do it! The more
you do it, the more comfortable you will be. When you
see how much fun it is and how appreciative others are for
the invitation, it will spur you on to greatness in your own
hospitality ministry.

Tim and I lived in Colorado Springs for five of the first
seven years of our marriage. Our first year there, we lived

in an apartment and began building a home. I told myself
that after we got into our nice, new home, I would invite
others over for dinner. All our friends had nice homes,
and I was embarrassed we were in an apartment. The
time came when we were in our new home, yet I always
found an excuse for not inviting others over. I realized it
wasn't the fact that we were in an apartment before; it was
a heart issue. I was intimidated by others and afraid to
attempt cooking or extend hospitality to them. I knew it
was an excuse and failed to see what God's Word said
about being hospitable.

Have you ever said to someone, "We should get together
sometime," and then never follow through? The first step
is to invite someone over and pick a date at the same time.
This way you both get it on your calendar and the date is
set. It saves you from the responsibility of remembering
to call and set the date later. We get busy and forget or
chicken out if we are new at it. Give yourself ample time
to prepare and plan. Unless you happen to be one of those
people who are able to keep a spotless house all the time,
you'll want extra time to clean and prepare a meal. I used
to consider myself a very particular housekeeper; then, I
had eight children! Yes, I need ample time to do extra
cleaning before inviting guests into my home.

I recommend that you put a planning page together in
advance of things that need to be done before guests
arrive. Include things such as a written menu of what you
are serving, how long it will take to prepare each item, and
when to thaw and/or marinate meat. Also include other
home preparations such as mow the lawn, clean the
house, and make sure you have propane if using a gas grill.

Don't be afraid of small beginnings. If fixing a full meal is
out of the question at times for you, invite someone over
for desert or small snack, and plan to have a nice time of

fellowship. Be teachable and recruit help from a friend or family member that is comfortable in the area of hospitality.

You may be asking who you should invite to your home. **Luke 14:12-14** tells us, **"When you give a dinner or a supper, do not ask your friends, your brothers, your relatives, or your rich neighbors, lest they also invite you back and you be repaid. But when you give a feast, invite the poor, the maimed, the lame, the blind. And you will be blessed; because they cannot repay you; for you shall be repaid at the resurrection of the just."** Always keep in mind, the purpose is to show love and serve God by serving others; this is the essence of hospitality. The scripture does not say that you shouldn't invite your friends and family. We know keeping friends and good family relationships comes by spending time together. The gist of the message is to invite others, who can't repay you, as an opportunity to love and serve with the right heart-attitude, knowing some are unable to do anything for you. A real heart of love serves others without expectations of getting something in return. This is love with no strings attached!

During our time in Colorado, we were invited many times to share Thanksgiving with other families in our church. What a great blessing this was for the two of us since I didn't know the first thing about cooking a Thanksgiving turkey with all the trimmings. One year, while pregnant with our first child, we had not received an invite to dinner, so we decided to patronize the local cafeteria. It was there that I consumed the worst Thanksgiving meal I had ever eaten. All the turkey gravy was gone, so I ate brown gravy with my dinner. This might not seem like a big deal to you, but to me, it was awful. Couple that with the fact that I was experiencing morning sickness at the time and you have the makings of the worst meal I can ever remember eating. As a result of that situation, Thanksgiving now provides my family each year with an opportunity to show hospitality to those in and beyond our circle of friends who may not have family around or are unable to offer a sufficient Thanksgiving meal to their families. We average approximately 40 people each year in our 1900-square foot home. We love it! People sit everywhere; tables are set up in my living, family, and dining rooms with a small table in the entry way. When people offer, I let them contribute to the meal but typically I fix an over-abundance of food. I love sharing the blessings God has given us throughout the year via the garden, fruit trees, berries, and hunting and fishing trips, as well as all the traditional Thanksgiving entrees.

The holidays provide great opportunities to bless and minister to others in tangible ways. Due to the fact many are lonely during this time, it's a great way to be a friend and put joy back into discouraged or disappointed hearts. We have also started doing an Open House the last Sunday evening before Christmas. People come and go as they wish, enjoying homemade goodies, beverages, and mostly a warm greeting and fellowship in our home. This allows me the joy of baking mounds of goodies and snacks without having them all to eat myself!

You may think this sounds overwhelming and you could never do it yourself but if I can learn, so can you. Don't be afraid of failure or intimidation. Just ask God to help you, and then jump in and do it. Practice may not always make perfect, but it does increase your skill. Determine today that you will discipline yourself to a lifestyle of exercising your gift of hospitality. Make that call, schedule that date, and enjoy the fellowship! And, as the scripture in Luke says, God will repay you for it at the resurrection. What a wonderful way to lay up treasures to your account in Heaven! **BE GIVEN TO HOSPITALITY!**

Tag from Tim, a husband's perspective:

While dating, Debbie made a fruit pie to impress me. In all seriousness, it was more like a giant pop tart. I tease her about it to this day, but trúly she has turned into an amazing cook and makes remarkable pies. Occasionally I have people over from the church for a meeting. Debbie graciously prepares a light meal, including a variety of soups, homemade bread, and fresh baked cookies. This is one of my favorite meals, and you should hear the raves as people taste the different soups. It really is fun, so try it out sometime; your friends will love it.

Home Care and Decorating

Why is it you can visit a beautifully decorated house yet return to your own home and fall into that favorite chair feeling perfectly content, even if it doesn't compare to the one you just left? When Tim and I lived in Colorado Springs, we were invited to dinner by a couple from our church. They had recently purchased a new home and beautiful furnishings to go with it. Upon arrival for our visit, we removed our shoes, and she promptly bypassed the living room, taking us into the kitchen. Our host explained that they didn't use their living room, and she even backed out of the room when vacuuming in order to not leave any footprints in the carpet. At the time I thought how wonderful it must be to have a home so perfect with enough room that you don't have to use all of it, enabling you to keep it spotless. That may work for some people but as I look back now, I think how crazy it would be for me personally to have a clean, well decorated home with beautiful furniture that I won't use for fear it won't stay perfect. Why own something that serves no purpose? Your home has a wonderful purpose! It's a place of nurturing, rest, peace, hospitality, and love—a place where your children grow up learning and where your husband loves returning to from work each day.

Our homes should be places that feel warm, inviting, and very peaceful. They should reflect who we are, our personalities. We desire that our guests feel at home when they walk in the front door, not fearful of messing something up. Home should be well maintained and orderly with an atmosphere that says, "Come, sit, relax, and have a moment of peace and rest." This type of atmosphere can be created through cleanliness and lack of clutter.

Cleanliness is important if you want people to be comfortable in your home. I can remember a story about a family who went to someone's home for an Italian dinner, only to discover that the host rolled the pasta out on her kitchen floor. Did I mention she had a family dog that lived inside? Again, for some of you, that may not be an issue, but to the average person, this would be reason enough NOT to partake of the meal. I encourage you to be sensitive to the guests you are inviting and aware of any pet allergies or cleanliness issues that might surface due to animals kept inside the home.

My husband performed a wedding ceremony for a couple in which the groom had completed chef's school and was preparing dinner for about 50 people at the reception. He brought all his own dishes from home. However, one look at these dishes told me even if I decided not to eat, they must be washed again. I proceeded to wash them all by hand and knowing the cleanliness situation, opted out of eating the food, too.

I share these stories not to be critical but to help you understand that if your home is not clean, it will be difficult for guests to relax and enjoy the hospitality you are extending to them. This doesn't mean it should always have to pass the *white glove test*, but it should look clean and smell fresh.

A home that is too cluttered can represent a life of chaos. I can remember another incident of going to someone's home for dinner, and having never been there before, I was a little surprised. Understanding the home was small, there was so much stuff that we barely had a path to walk around furniture and clutter. I felt claustrophobic. Our host led us around the entire place showing off each room and all her collectables. There were literally thousands of little trinkets sitting throughout the home on every piece of furniture imaginable. Her home spoke to who she was, her personality, but it was so congested we could hardly enjoy the time spent there. I think we all breathed a sigh of relief upon leaving. The atmosphere felt busy, chaotic; no peace or relaxation there, only a feeling of, "It must be time to go!" Something more simplistic speaks of order and tidiness!

I recommend you scour your home for any extra clutter that serves no purpose or has no special meaning. We have a tendency to hold on to things long after the novelty wears off, or, in the event that someone gave us a gift, we don't want to hurt their feelings by disposing of it. Tell yourself that it's really okay. Keep things for a season but don't feel bad about getting rid of or giving away items that are no longer useful to you. This will go a long way in de-cluttering your home.

The more things you have sitting around to look at, the longer it takes you to clean. You can optimize your cleaning time by de-cluttering your home. Have you hung onto things you used to collect but don't anymore? Now would be a good time to think about selling them to other collectors if they are taking up space and don't have a lot of value to you anymore. I used to collect spoons when I went on trips. After many years, I decided it wasn't that important to me so I gave away all but those I collected overseas on a tour of Israel.

Tim and I have been homeschooling our children for 18 years. In the past few years, we began making the transition for our older children to attend public school, some full time and some part time. During this transition, I realized there was an abundance of books in my bookcase and file cabinet that would no longer be used. Although we could have sold many of them for money, we chose to give boxes away to two families that were homeschooling their children while on the road traveling and ministering. This was an opportunity to give toward these wonderful ministries and de-clutter my home at the same time.

I have discovered as my kids got older, they needed more space. They personally take up more room, and so do their clothes. I understand how difficult it is to put a large family such as ours into a moderate sized home. We have a 1,900-square foot, four-bedroom home. That leaves one bedroom for us and three for eight kids. Due to the fact we only have one daughter who is old enough to need extra privacy, we had five boys in one bedroom and two in another for a while before they started leaving for college. Bunk beds are a wonderful invention! You *can* make space work for you and accommodate however many children you have. The difficult part is keeping things orderly with so many people in so little space.

The first thing to remember is your home won't stay perfectly clean; I repeat, it will be nearly impossible to have a spotless home with little ones! **Proverbs 14:4 says, "Where no oxen are, the trough is clean."** This is not to say our children are oxen; just if there are kids in the house, the *trough* might get a little dirty. Give yourself a lot of grace, and don't expect perfection from your husband, your kids, or yourself. DO, however, train them continually to pick up after themselves and take on

household responsibilities. This training WILL NOT
happen overnight; it will take a lifetime.

When decorating your home, let it reflect the things you
like and what's important to you. For example, you may
have furnishings which look like yard sale items but are
comfortable, practical, and may have sentimental value.
It's always a good idea to look for ways to spruce up these
pieces, and that's part of the fun. Be creative with throws,
linens, and pillows. I was given my grandmother's old
sewing bench and box after she passed away. Most people
would think nothing of them, but to me they are treasures.
They remind me of my grandmother who sewed my
wedding dress. The box is strictly for décor but I have a
blanket thrown over the bench to keep it from getting
worn, while still using it for practical purposes. I have
many pieces of wood furniture, most of which are different
types and grains of wood. I personally like the diversity of
wood grains and colors in my house. You may prefer to
stick with only one. Choose what you like and what
reflects your style.

Our family room furniture was purchased shortly after we
got married 27 years ago. My children think it's ancient
but the fact is that 27 years of marriage and eight kids
later, it's still standing and very useable. A few years ago I
purchased a couple of matching throws to cover the
wearing cushions. Using my husband's bear rug and other
nature-looking décor, I created a comfortable, rustic
atmosphere, used as a place to lounge on the couch, play
games, watch movies, and kick our feet up without
worrying about hurting expensive furniture. This truly is a
family room!

Take a look at what you have and be creative. Don't think
for a moment that you have to purchase new furniture to

decorate your home. You might be surprised at what you can find laying around the house to work with.

For years, Tim and I have been contemplating what to do with the kitchen. After purchasing our home 8 years ago, we made some desperately-needed repairs and upgrades, including flooring and paint. We saved out enough money from what we had for our down payment to do these projects since the house needed a little TLC. Unfortunately, with the high cost of kitchen cabinets and countertops, we couldn't upgrade this part of the home. It would have cost us in the neighborhood of $10,000, which definitely was not in the budget. As I do on occasion, I got a "wild hair" to refinish all the cabinets. With a little elbow grease, stain, and lots of patience, I began the project. We ended up redoing not just the kitchen cabinets but all the bathroom cabinets too. To complete the project, we painted a wall and accent areas to give the kitchen an entirely new look. After two weeks of non-stop work, we completed the job, all for under $200, and the kitchen looks brand new. The difference in stain color even made the old countertops look better.

Fresh paint can do wonders for your home, including changing the atmosphere of a room from drab to fun or warm-feeling. How wonderful it is to do a project that gives your home a new, fresh look and spend a fraction of the cost of purchasing new or having the work done by a professional. If you aren't afraid to get a little dirty and potentially *break a nail*, you can learn to do creative upgrades to your home and spend very little money doing it! There is such satisfaction in seeing a job completed knowing you had a part in it.

If you are like me and prefer the wood grain on a table to show but want to protect the top, I recommend you go to a local store and purchase the needed length of clear vinyl to cover your table. This protects the top of the table, is easy to clean, and allows the beauty of the wood to show through. Another thing I did was to purchase enough of this vinyl to cover the cloth cushions on our chairs. This makes after dinner clean up easy and keeps the cloth on the chairs from getting soiled and eventually ruined. If you have kids and have ever bought cloth-covered, dining room chairs, you will greatly appreciate this advice.

In the living room, an open book with a pair of glasses and a candle or lamp can dress up any table; simple, yet elegant at the same time. I have found that rolling up extra towels and standing them in basket in the bathroom is a neat and attractive way to keep extra towels handy and available. I use the open space on the top of kitchen cabinets to set all my canning supplies (some antique), an ice cream bucket, and extra large pots that won't fit under the cabinet. This will give your kitchen a homey aura. Not only are they decorative, they are also very useful items that are easily accessible.

The holidays can be challenging for those of us who aren't great decorators, but let me share with you my favorite thoughts on preparing your home for the season. Simplicity is usually a good rule of thumb. Extra lights, fresh garland, candles or other soft lights, and holiday smells will go a long way. Buy lights at the end of the season on clearance, and store them for the next year. You will spend a fraction of the money. I really like the new LED candles recently on the market; they look like a candle burning but without the danger of fire or getting burned.

I think my number one advice is to keep the focus of your home about Jesus, so your children will know who and why you celebrate. If you decorate a Christmas tree, make certain it's not the central focus. I like to set up a nativity with my Bible laid open to the Christmas story in Luke chapter 2. With a light shining on it, this nativity has become the focus in our home over the holidays. It's what we set packages around so our children know it's all about the birth of a wonderful Savior, not a beautifully decorated tree. It's easy to cause confusion in the minds of our children by having most everything secular and very little about why we celebrate Christmas in the first place. Let them know that the life of Jesus is the very best reason to celebrate, and we are going to celebrate life in Him...in a BIG way!

These are very basic ideas that I have shared; nothing profound but tips that can give you a good start to cleaning and caring for your home in order to create an atmosphere that speaks of who you are. I think the most important thing to remember is to be yourself, and if you like it, use it. It's your home, and you know what your family likes better than any decorator! **HAPPY DECORATING!**

Tag from Tim, a husband perspective:

With eight males under one roof you can imagine what gets dragged in from time to time. I really appreciate the patience Debbie displays toward our *weird guy quirks*. At the same time I love a clean, tidy home, a place which has that warm feel, a safe haven, a place of peace in a busy world. What sets our home apart from others? It's not extravagant furnishings or the finest of china; it's that everything is done with LOVE. I think love makes food taste better and transforms our house into an awesome home.

Train Up a Child

I am completely convinced that parenting *is* the most difficult job on the planet. It has been calculated how much a woman should earn being a stay-at-home mom based on all the things she does and the knowledge she has to obtain...the amount, you ask?; About $110,000 dollars per year, triple-digit income; a healthy amount for any profession. If only you could get your hands on that money, right? When you pour your heart and soul into your family, you are working 24/7, just like the perception we have of the Proverbs 31 woman. The real truth of the matter is, even a million dollars per year wouldn't come close to paying the salary of a person that can change the world based on her ability to train her children. You are priceless!

Third John, verse 4 tells us, "I have no greater joy than to hear that my children walk in truth." Have you considered the depth of that passage? It tells us there is nothing that blesses me and gives me greater joy than to know my children have embraced the truth of God's Word. They are serving Him with their whole hearts and have a personal relationship with the almighty God and King of the universe. We can be assured that if walking in truth, our children won't be living a lie or straying down the wrong path. That's good news; news that fills you with unspeakable joy; the greatest joy in the world!

Consider for a moment, the opposite of this scripture. It could very well be said, "I have no greater heartache than to hear that my children are *not* walking in truth." For many mothers, this is closer to reality. They are mothers living their greatest heartache everyday due to the fact their children aren't serving the Lord. To you that fall into this category, never give up on them. Pray in faith continually and know that God has them in His sights. Just as the father of the prodigal saw his son from afar off, so our Heavenly Father sees us when we stray. There is absolutely no place we can go away from God's presence. He is always there! He sees your child. Have faith and keep believing for them...eternity depends on praying mothers!

I haven't been a perfect mother, far from it. I've made many mistakes; however, from 22 years of child-training, I have learned to be transparent with my children and share my life with them. From the time my first son was still a toddler, people would tell me what wonderful kids I have. I also had many others tell me, "Just wait till they are teenagers!" Then when they became teens, people said to me, "You just got lucky having such good kids." I told those complimenting me that it was the grace of God, and it was! However, I learned an incredibly important precept in scripture. **Proverbs 22:6 says, "Train up a child in the way he should go and when he is old, he will not depart from it."** (NKJV)

There are some very critical points to pull from this passage. First of all, the word train shows action. The definition of train is: to form by instruction and discipline; to make fit, qualified and proficient; to aim. We are responsible for instructing our children in the knowledge we desire them to have. We discipline them by encouraging good behavior and correcting poor behavior. Preparing them for adulthood requires a great amount of effort on our part. We must aim them in the right direction, making them fit and qualified to be productive at whatever occupation or ministry God has for them.

If I could summarize child-training into one statement it would be: **MORE IS CAUGHT THAN TAUGHT!** It is a well-known fact that when grown, children model the behaviors of their parents. Children will learn our behaviors more than our words. We must model character and integrity in every area of our lives. Whatever character we want them to display, we must live *it* before them—for them!

Matthew 7:16-17 says, **"You will know them by their fruit...every good tree bears good fruit, but a bad tree bears bad fruit."** (NKJ) Good or bad, we are known by the fruit we bear. If we want good fruit from our children, we must bear good fruit ourselves. Model the Fruit of the Spirit before them: love, joy, peace, patience, kindness, goodness, faithfulness, gentleness, and self-control.

One of my greatest battles has been a spirit of negativity. It seemed I was always looking for the bad in every situation rather than the good, picking out the faults of others rather than their strong points. My grandmother battled it, my mother battled it, and I battle it. It is what I remember modeled for me; it's what my mother remembers modeled for her. My grandmother is with Jesus now, but my mother and I have conversed many times on the subject and how this has been such a difficult area for each of us to overcome. We have both made progress, and with the help of God and my family, I will be an overcomer. Transparency with my children and husband regarding this issue has allowed each of them to hold me accountable.

Don't be afraid of transparency, and if you have an area in your life that needs accountability, allow your children and husband to play a part. Let me just interject that there are some areas of accountability which should be reserved for your spouse only. This might include addictions or other destructive behaviors. The idea here is to have all the accountability you need to be the model parent God wants you to be! Share your ups and downs with your children, and most importantly, let them see you responding in love toward each situation. Let them see you loving and showing kindness to those who haven't loved and showed kindness to you, patience when you don't want to wait, compassion to others regardless of their situation, and forgiveness no matter the offense. By doing such, you will train up godly, compassionate, forgiving, loving, and kind children.

Another good rule of thumb to train by is **ALWAYS MAKE BAD BEHAVIOR COUNTER-PRODUCTIVE** and **MEAN WHAT YOU SAY!** Make certain your children understand that nothing will be gained by poor behavior. If they are whiney and demanding, let them know that because of it, they will not be given what they want. Tell them to try asking correctly later, and if their request meets your qualifications, bless them with it. This will correct the behavior and teach them to be patient, waiting for something they really want. Don't indulge your children every time they ask for something. Your child's birthday and Christmas provides a great opportunity to surprise them with gifts they have wanted for months, and in a child's eyes, that's a really long time! This may sound like an oversimplification, and really it is. However, it is foundational to training up well-mannered, obedient, and patient children.

If you instruct your children to clean their room, then mean it and expect it. I heard a lady say once years ago, "You can't expect what you don't inspect!" You can't expect a clean room if you don't inspect it to see if it got cleaned. If they are told to stop throwing a tantrum, then expect them to stop. My children were told they could cry when hurt but never out of anger and never while screaming.

It is a wise mother that will train her children to act at home the same way she expects them to behave in public. When our oldest son, Ben, was about six months old, we went with friends out to dinner. As our salads were served, Ben's hand went right for my plate, and he proceeded to launch salad all over me and the restaurant as far as he could throw. He may have been just a baby, but I had to see this as a training opportunity. A little slap on the back of his hand, a firm no, and being pulled back from the table was all it took. He didn't attempt to grab our plates again. As Senior Pastors of a church, we are accustomed to taking guest speakers and missionaries out to dinner or to our home following services. We would tell our children, "We are dining with guest so be on your best behavior!" It occurred to me one day that this was poor training. What it told my children was, "I don't have to exercise good behavior and table manners all the time, only when we are with guests!" After that, I started saying, "Be on your best behavior...as always!" I have learned, after nearly ten years of having teenagers in my home, that most of the time our kids will live up to the expectations we have of them. If we expect and model good behavior, we will get it in return.

Many mothers I speak with battle *yelling* at their children. I know of no other behavior more difficult to control than this. When my sixth son was a baby, I was working hard at controlling my tendency to yell at my children. Tim and I were out of town attending a pastors' conference when he rounded a corner in our van, and my water spilled on the floor. It just so happened that his Bible was also on the floor between the seats, getting wet. Tim's

instant reaction was to yell at me to pick up his Bible so it
would not get wetter than it already was. While feeling
offended and upset with him for yelling at me, the Lord
prompted my spirit saying, "This is how your children feel
when you yell at them." My heart instantly broke with
repentance, and afterward, it was much easier to
overcome this issue I had dealt with for many years. God
used that situation for my good, so I could stop this
offense I was committing against my children. If we as
mothers can see and understand how degrading it is to be
yelled at, it will help us be overcomers in this area of our
lives. We don't want to degrade our children; we want to
build them up with the Word of God.

Deuteronomy 6:6-9 tells us, **"And these words which I
command you today shall be in your heart; you shall
teach them diligently to your children, and shall talk
of them when you sit in your house, when you walk
by the way, when you lie down, and when you rise up.
You shall bind them as a sign on your hand, and they
shall be as frontlets between your eyes. You shall
write them on the doorposts of your house and on
your gates."** The obvious implication with this passage is
that we should be intentional about training our children
in the ways of the Lord. It should be a lifestyle, not just
something we do occasionally. We live it, walk it, breathe
it, and talk it with our children all the time. They must
see us live it out before them and speak God's Word into
their lives.

I can remember when my third son Josiah was four years
old. We were driving down the road having a deep,
theological discussion about God and Heaven, when Joey
piped up and said, "Yeah, we have to love Jesus because if
we don't, we go to Hell and get all fired up!" Out of the
mouth of babes! Though his perception was a little
skewed, he was pretty accurate in his analysis. Don't miss

opportunities to share God's Word with your children.
Use everyday situations in the lives of your family and
friends to share the truth of scripture with these little ones
God gave you. Their very lives depend on it! Teach them
to memorize scripture, hiding it in their heart that they
would refrain from sinning against God and His Word.

Finally, I encourage you to *commit* your children to the
Lord. **II Timothy 1:12a, "… for I know whom I have
believed and am persuaded that He is able to keep
what I have committed to Him until that day."** You
can rest assured that if you commit your children to the
Lord, do all you know to do to train them, and ask for
wisdom from God who gives it liberally to those who ask,
He *is* able to keep them! Pray for them constantly, stand
fast on God's Word, believe what He says, and should they
struggle for a time, know your children are always in His
care and will return to what they know is truth! **I believe
it *and* I've lived it!**

Tag from Tim, a husband's perspective:

Preacher's kids (PKs) are typically stereotyped as being the
rowdiest, most obnoxious kids on the planet and I have
known some to live up to that expectation. I can think of
three reasons why PK's have a tendency to walk away from
God for a time. 1) PK's are typically under the microscope
at church, or at least they feel the pressure, whether it is
real or perceived. 2) I tend to believe that parents often
set a double standard; one for home and one for church.
3) Because church and family in a pastor's home are so
closely knit, when trouble or stressful situations arise, the
entire family is often impacted. On the surface, these
seem like insurmountable odds; however, I believe these
obstacles can be overcome by three distinct approaches. 1)
You establish the expectation for your children through
God's Word, not allowing anyone else to dictate their

expectations on your children. 2) Consistent parenting is a
key. Never set a double standard of living based on the
environment. In other words, hold your children to the
same expectation at home as you do at church. Debbie
even went so far as to have quiet time at home to prepare
the kids to sit in church and remain quiet, not fidgeting
during service. 3) We often instruct our children that we
cannot control what other people do or say in the church;
however we can control our response. So in every
situation a godly response is the target. Yes, we have all
missed the mark from time to time but our kids know that
is the exception and not the rule. Lastly, let me encourage
you to fight for your kids through prayer. There is nothing
more powerful than spending time everyday praying for
your family and calling your children out to God by name.
I believe prayer is the primary reason we have our three
oldest kids in active ministry today and the others on their
way to realizing their personal calling from God.

Cooking - It's a Piece of Cake!

Years ago a young lady was referred to me who needed help; she didn't know how to cook. This was hard for me to believe, but since that time, I have come to realize it's definitely more the norm. If you fall into this category, I trust this chapter will challenge you to break open the recipe book and start cookin'!

The young lady I just mentioned sat with me for a couple of hours and shared how in two years of marriage, they were in credit card debt of over $20,000 due to eating out every meal. Another couple came to me asking for help in reducing their monthly grocery bill. They were a family of four, spending $2,000 a month on groceries. The husband was making a triple-digit income per year, but as the market started taking a downturn, so did his business. They were accustomed to eating many packaged foods, including boxed snacks and pre-packaged beverages. The wife didn't know where to start when it came to cooking and preparing meals from scratch and shopping on a budget. At the time I met with them, I was spending $500 a month on groceries for a family of ten. Since then, even with a couple of kids away at college part time, my food bill increased due to the rising costs at the grocery store. Looking back at our expenses for last year, we discovered $637 per month was spent on groceries which equates to two dollars per day, per person for meals. The average American family of four in 2009 spent $734 per month on meals. It *is* possible to lower your food bill and eat well at the same time.

My first advice to these families was to decide as a family that things were going to change and what everyone was accustomed to eating would be different. The snack cupboard will not be full of packaged junk food, and the canned beverages will be limited. There will definitely be a learning curve for mom as she starts cooking things from scratch, sometimes succeeding and sometimes really bombing! Have you ever heard the saying, "Tis a lesson you should heed: try, try again! If at first you don't succeed: try, try again; then your courage should appear, for if you will persevere; you will conquer never fear: try, try again!" That needs to be your motto. You just keep trying until you start gaining success. Everything you attempt to make will most likely not be perfect the first time. Perfection rarely comes for me, even after cooking from scratch for over 27 years. It's good but not always perfect.

I can remember the first time I tried making homemade, whole wheat bread. It was like a brick when it came out of the oven. I was so disappointed that while trying to cut through it with a knife, I did a karate chop on the bread only to have my finger in the way, cutting it wide open. It bled for hours but I refused to go get stitches; I was mad and definitely embarrassed over the whole episode. Years later, I decided to try my hand at bread again, and using the right equipment and exhibiting a lot of patience, I have nearly mastered bread making. One Saturday, we took our children to a lake for a day of fishing and picnicking. I was out of homemade bread so made a quick run to the store for a loaf. When I pulled out sandwich stuff at the lake, the kids noticed the bread was *from the store* and decided to go hungry rather than eat *store-bought bread*. My mother-in-law informed me I was spoiling them with the really good stuff, and they might never find wives to please them. She was right! Therefore today, with some talking to and training, they are more tolerant to eating *food from the store*!

Early in our marriage when I was buying products like Hamburger Helper, I made a "Cheeseburger Bake" that was unfit to eat. Since we wouldn't consume it, I fed it to our German Shepherd because he ate everything. Well, I should say I tried to feed it to Sampson, but he wouldn't eat it either. Now I have on my cooking record something *even the dog wouldn't eat!* That was the end of the pre-packaged main course for me! I had other less-successful attempts. My very first pie I made went on record for being a *pop-tart*; I failed to put enough pie filling in the crust. Now, my husband tells me I make excellent pies.

If I can learn to cook, then you can too. If you are determined to learn and be the very best you can be for your family, you will heed the little saying...try, try again; persevere and conquer. If you have a real *flop*, just know you are in good company, and the next try will be better. You will be amazed at what you can make, and your family will love you for it. Not only will you save money, but you'll eat healthier too.

One of the first things you should do, if cooking meals from scratch is new to you, is take inventory and make sure you have proper pans and utensils to cook with. Purchasing needed items is still cheaper than eating out or buying expensive pre-packaged food. I have a few items that I couldn't live without when cooking: crock pot, Bosch bread machine (heavy duty mixer), cast iron skillets, canner, and pressure cooker. I will discuss canning in a later chapter.

Meal planning is a must if you are new at cooking from scratch. It will help you ensure all ingredients and supplies are on hand before you ever begin a meal. My suggestion would be to get a calendar you can write on. Using a free calendar from business advertising is a good way to go; it's cheap, and you'll eventually throw it away. Then, think of your family's favorite foods and how often you like to eat them, maybe once a week. Write it in on the dates you choose; then think of other things like Mexican, Italian, or grilling. You could come up with four different Mexican dishes such as tacos, enchiladas, burritos, and chili nachos or taco salads and plug in one a week for the month. Do the same with Italian Meals such as spaghetti, lasagna, fettuccini Alfredo, and homemade pizza; plug these into the calendar. You can grill all winter even if it's cold, so how about ribs, burgers, steaks, and chicken. Write these into your calendar once a week. Maybe you could plan one night each week to try new recipes, and you now have five nights per week covered on your meal plan. Sundays are a great day for me to prepare dinner in the crock pot; plan on fixing roast, ham, Salisbury steak, and pork for four different Sunday dinners. You now have only one night a week to plan meals. This is a good time to use up leftovers or fix soup, specialty salads, or something else you prefer eating more than once a month.

You may have certain days of the week where faster prep is necessary and other days when you have more time to cook and can plan accordingly. Keep your schedule in mind when planning your monthly menu. If there is one day a week I always disliked cooking, it was Sunday. Trying to pull a quick dinner together by the time we arrived home from service was difficult. Something that has been very helpful to me is prepping Sunday's dinner on Saturday evening. I lay meat out of the freezer to thaw, make my salads, cut my potatoes, and cover with water in a pot or measure out rice if that's on the menu instead. Making a dessert on Saturday gives your family a sweet treat with Sunday dinner. You can put your frozen meat in the crock-pot, add the rest of the ingredients, and then by morning, your meat is thawed and ready for the pot to be turned on. There are great recipes available in books and online for the crock pot; I highly recommend you check them out. This will be a great help to you on busy days.

If you have family members or friends that are great cooks or have good organizational skills, ask them for a little time to meet with you and share their wisdom. They could teach you how to make their specialties, and working side-by-side with a friend is a lot of fun. You learn and have great fellowship all at the same time.

Don't be afraid to try preparing entrees without a recipe. Once you are comfortable with cooking, you will find it's a lot of fun trying and creating different foods. Be creative with leftovers, using them to make soup with leftover meat, vegetables, and rice or potatoes. Season with a little broth, add bread and salad, and you have a really fast, hot meal on a cold winter day. Plus you have used up food that would not have made another full meal but all combined, was just the right amount for a pot of soup. You save money and don't waste leftovers! How sweet is that!

You will find many of my favorite recipes in the recipe chapter, as well as tips for canning in a later chapter. If you use this guide, you will be making home cooked meals that taste better than anything you could ever get in a package or at a restaurant. The only problem is your husband may not want to eat in a restaurant ever again because he married you! **HAPPY COOKIN'!**

Tag from Tim, a husband's perspective:

What can I say? I rather enjoy my food, especially eating
at home. On occasion I travel for various meetings. All
too soon I am looking forward to being home and eating
Debbie's cooking and spending time with my family. I
really appreciate the fact Debbie knows how to stretch the
food budget while still offering the family quality meals
and something to satisfy my sweet tooth.

Mom Care – Take Time to Take Care!

You can't give what you don't have! Recently I went through a period of time when I told my husband, "I had nothing left to give but up!" A busy schedule of teaching, studying, writing, planning multiple events in a row, and trying to keep up on the busyness of home and church, had me completely exhausted. Although everything on my schedule dealt with ministry to others, there was little or no strength left in me to do so. I have to remind myself frequently that, contrary to public opinion, I am NOT Wonder Woman, Mrs. Incredible, or anyone else that can go non-stop without breaking to care for herself. *I must take time to take care!*

There is a very strong implication in this phrase that speaks of intentionality and personal responsibility. As homemakers, wives, mothers, and ministers, we must take responsibility to care for ourselves, or we will slip into total exhaustion, having nothing left to give our families or others. Personally, I strongly dislike wasting time. It has been ingrained in me my entire life to wake up early, work hard, and go to bed at a decent hour, so I'm ready to start another day. It has been driven into my DNA to work diligently and accomplish much in a day; life is too short to waste any of it on idleness. I'm certain many of you feel the same, but I want to encourage you in the fact that *idleness* and *rest* are two completely different things.

First of all, the literal definition of *idleness* is doing nothing—useless, ineffective, or fruitless; *whereas rest* is the refreshing quiet of sleep and the relief from anything that wearies, troubles, or disturbs us. How I wish I had understood this concept when I was younger. Idleness is doing nothing when there's work to be done; rest is taking a break from the normal pace of hard work. Please understand that resting your body, mind, and spirit are critical to maintaining your *whole* being for the long haul. We must pace ourselves if we expect to live long, healthy lives, doing great things for the Kingdom of God through serving our families. For our own physical, spiritual, and emotional well being, we *must*, **"take time to take care!"** Let's take a look first at caring for our Spirit. When we find ourselves at the point of total exhaustion, the point where we are "exhausted to tears" (some of you have experienced this when you are so tired, having only the strength to cry), the first thing to do is go to God. Cry out to Him according to His Word:

"Hear my cry, O God; attend to my prayer. From the end of the earth I will cry to You, when my heart is overwhelmed, lead me to the rock that is higher than I.

For You have been a shelter for me and a strong tower from the enemy. I will abide in Your tabernacle forever; I will trust in the shelter of Your wings.

For you O God have heard my vows; You have given me the heritage of those who fear Your name. You will prolong my life, my years as many generations. I shall abide before God forever. Oh, prepare mercy and truth, which may preserve me!

So I will sing praise to your name forever, that I may daily perform my vows!"

(Psalm 61:1-8)

When I am overwhelmed with life, I cry out to my Lord, and He will lead me to that place, a refuge much higher than I. It is a place of shelter, protection, and defense against the enemy; a place where I am preserved to ultimately perform my vows or calling. It is when we are the most tired that we begin to feel disconnected from God and other relationships. This leaves us vulnerable to the enemy's advances and schemes. God has a place of refuge for us if we will go to Him. Commit yourself to the spiritual disciplines of reading and studying God's Word plus spending time in prayer and meditation every day. You will find this daily habit to be life and breath, fresh living water to a dry and thirsty spirit.

Emotional unsteadiness in our life can also stem from exhaustion. As a woman, my emotions are so interconnected with my hormones, which rely on a healthy, rested body to function correctly. Without proper rest, my emotions and hormones can, and likely will, operate like an electrical storm in my body with hot wires running everywhere. This is the point where we have emotion-based outbursts and get depressed over day-to-day issues of life.

We can look at examples in God's Word of those who experienced great victories at the hand of God yet moments later had drifted into great depression and wanted their life to end due to total exhaustion. Elijah is a great example of this. Following his great victory against the prophets of Baal on Mount Carmel, Elijah walked one day's journey into the wilderness, sat down under a tree, and asked God to let him die. While he slept, an angel came to him saying, "Rise and eat," which he did. This food and rest carried him another 40 days. WOW, what a little rest and proper eating will do to change our perspective and attitude on life! Our emotions are dependent upon proper rest and healthy food. Take care to eat healthy and get ample sleep every night so you are rested and energized for each day's work.

Physical well being is the final area I want to cover in this chapter. Again, rest is crucial to a healthy body. Our bones, muscles, brain, and whole internal system desperately need rest and proper care to work as they ought. Ignoring car problems will eventually cause vehicles to break down; the same goes for our bodies. Learn to pay attention to how your body feels and respond appropriately. If you feel tired, you need rest. If you feel hungry, you likely need to eat. Chronic tiredness can also be a symptom of dehydration. Make certain you keep hydrated daily. My son had a Junior High football coach who used to say, "Hydrate today for a better tomorrow." He understood the concept that keeping your body hydrated will allow it to function well every day.

Daily physical exercise is another important discipline to keep us healthy and increase our energy, strength, and stamina. It's good for the physical and emotional well-being, as well as providing an opportunity to take in and memorize God's Word, building up the spirit while you exercise. If you are one of many who struggle in the area of weight management, then exercise and healthy eating will be critical to you. It *is* possible to lose weight and get healthy! With a little determination and a lot of God's help, you can get your whole being back in balance. It *is* the temple of the Holy Ghost, and we ought to treat it as such.

It is easy to see, looking at all these things that if we want wholeness in our life, we must be intentional about taking care of ourselves. Nearly impossible is the task of ministering to others unless we *"Take Time to Take Care!"*

Tag from Tim, a husband's perspective:

You have probably heard the saying, "If you want something done ask a busy person." On the other hand the Message Bible says, "Husbands go all out in love for your wives. Don't take advantage of them." Col. 3:19 (The Message). At times I have been guilty of asking Debbie to do too much. She is so willing to help and serve that, if I am not careful, I will overwhelm her with responsibility. I concur with Debbie as usual! Your responsibilities are heavy, so please, take some time to rest and get rejuvenated.

Heart of a Servant

It happened that while in the midst of writing this book, God revealed to me a level of selfishness I was dealing with in my heart. We can be so busy in caring for children, our husband, and ourselves—not to mention all the other responsibilities women have—we forget our ministry to others.

Recently, we had our annual Church Family Camp. I planned the menu, shopped for the food, and prepared many items at home to take. The day before leaving, I anticipated going early to the office to study for the message I would preach the next evening at camp and expected to be home around noon to work on food preparation. I arrived at the office early to find my husband needing help with errands; I didn't get to work on my message until 10:00 a.m. As soon as I began to study, I received a call from a friend that was having difficulties dealing with pressing issues in her life. Depression was consuming her from many stressful, personal circumstances. I would spend the next hour and a half talking on the phone and lending a listening ear.

This was just the beginning of many distractions that would consume my time that day. I left for home at 4:00 p.m. having not done any studying or writing of my message. After arriving at home, I spent the following three hours making spaghetti sauce, salsa, granola, plum jam, and cooking dinner for my family, all the while cleaning house in preparation for the Bible Study I would teach in my home that evening. Somehow, by the grace of God, I got it all done and taught my class, but still no message was prepared for the next day.

Following Bible Study, I still had cookie dough to mix up for camp before I could work on a message. Finally at 10:00 p.m., I retired to my desk in my room and prepared to study. At that very moment, I got a text message regarding the same friend that said, "Can you please help her, she is really struggling!" I spent the next two hours texting encouragement, all the while trying to work on my message. Completing my sermon but not really knowing what I had written, I fell into bed sometime after 1:00 a.m. The alarm rang at 6:00 a.m; I hopped out of bed, got ready for my day, packed clothes for camp, put all the food together, and loaded the church trailer just in time to print off my message and leave for camp at 12:00 noon. I never had the opportunity to look over what I had written until about 5:00 p.m., and to top it off, it was a narrative message, which meant I needed to have it mostly memorized.

Never in my years of ministry and preaching had I ever felt so unprepared. I sensed frustration over all the distractions and those who had caused the distractions. Realizing the attitude behind my feelings, I needed to get alone with God and pray for the right heart and proper perspective in dealing with the many things I was frustrated over. Through this, God showed me an important value: PEOPLE ARE MORE IMPORTANT THAN MY TO-DO LIST...even when it came to ministry preparation! People have real needs; my list of to dos can wait, whereas sometimes people's needs can't.

Following Family Camp, I set a personal goal for myself regarding the completion of my first draft on this book. As the month progressed, I found that my goal had been unrealistic and even more than an unrealistic goal, people needed my attention, taking me away from critical writing time. My father was trying to re-roof his house and needed help. I committed to spending a couple of days helping to tear off the old roof and prep for a new one. The roofing material was hot, and after the first day, the palms of my hands and the tips of my fingers were covered in blisters—not from the hard work but from the heat. They hurt a little but through it, I remembered what God had told me...people are more important than my to-do list, and my dad needed the help. As I worked on the hot roof in one-hundred-degree temperatures, I spent time thanking God for the opportunity to help someone who had always been there for me and still is to this day! I saw this opportunity to serve my father as a blessing, not a distraction from my to-do list. Indeed people are so much more valuable than the list of things we think we have to get done. I missed my goal of completion on the book but I blessed someone with much needed time.

While I was on my dad's roof, I received a call from my husband who informed me someone we knew needed childcare for the following week, as she was hoping to go see family in another state. I cringed a little but remembered the word God spoke to me and consented to the task. Although her trip fell through and she didn't need childcare after all, I knew this was another test to see how well I had learned this valuable lesson.

The heart of a servant puts others needs ahead of their own. In everything we do, we must remember that people are all we can take to Heaven with us. The dishes, laundry, school, jobs, and so on, will all be left behind some day, but by the Grace of God, our families won't be!

Allow God to grow and stretch you, molding you into the servant He wants you to be. **Live life with a servant's heart, pursuing a servant's call!**

Tag from Tim, a husband's perspective:

To live love *with no strings attached* is as unnatural as Debbie tearing the roof off a house. Yet even beyond the blistering side effects, it's worth the price both now and forever. The Message Bible tells us to "Pursue the things over which Christ presides. Don't shuffle along, eyes to the ground, absorbed with the things right in front of you. Look up and be alert to what is going on around Christ – that's where the action is. See things from His perspective." Col 3:1-2 (The Message). The liberation movement in America was birthed in a sea of selfishness, and selfishness is the foundation of sin. The Word of God tells us to see life from a different perspective and live it to the fullest. Life's real satisfaction comes from living love *with no strings attached.*

Part Two

Practical Home Helps for the Domestic Diva

"I Think I *Can*, I Think I *Can*"

Remember the story of the Little Engine That Could?
With hard work and perseverance, he finally made it up
the mountain. Learning food preservation and how to *can*
is a little bit like that; it takes hard work and perseverance
to learn how to do it and actually get the job done. Facing
mountains of fruits and vegetables in the summer and
early fall takes a great deal of determination to complete,
all the while telling yourself, "I think I *can*, I think I *can!*"

Recently, I received a call from a single, young lady,
wanting to learn canning procedures. I told her I was
canning peaches and tomatoes if she wanted to come help
me. When she arrived at my home, I was at the kitchen
sink peeling peaches, wearing *work* clothes. My hair was a
mess. Deciding it was the thing to do, I warned her that
canning not only makes you look like a haggard
housewife, it makes you feel like one too! We both
laughed. Canning is definitely not for the weak, but it is
for every Domestic Diva who is willing to work hard to
preserve fresh fruits and veggies for the family to be used
in the months when fresh items are out of season.

If you have ever eaten home-grown, fresh produce, it
spoils you; you will never want to buy a tomato from the
grocery store again. They just aren't the same. By getting

freshly picked, quality produce in the summer, you can preserve good, healthy food for your family at a much reduced rate from purchasing canned items in the store. This allows you to save money and feed your family healthy foods. The best part is you know exactly what's going into the jars and freezer bags and how it was handled; whereas you're not privy to that information when buying off the store shelves.

There are a few items you will need to purchase which are necessary for canning. Depending on the foods you are doing, you will need: a canning guide, water bath canner, pressure cooker canner, juicer, freezer bags, jar lifter, canning funnel, and small tongs for lifting lids out of hot water. All of these items are available and can be purchased at your local store. You can purchase a canning kit with all the basic supplies included for around $50.00, but the pressure cooker canners are about double that price. Jars and lids can be purchased in most local grocery stores. I recommend to ladies that if they really want to pursue canning, ask for these items for birthday and Christmas gifts, or suggest that everyone give you money toward the purchase of these items. Another option is to regularly check second-hand stores for jars and canning supplies. Often you can pick them up for a fraction of the cost of buying new. They will become part of your kitchen basics and *must-have* items.

I also recommend getting the word out to everyone you know; many people quit canning when their kids move away from home, and they have jars and canners to get rid of. Once people learn you are looking for these items, you are likely to get donations coming your way. It is surprising the number of people that have gardens and fruit trees but don't use all the harvest. If they find out you can, getting free produce just for the picking is very likely. Check your local newspaper or even online ads; we have found free produce offered just for the picking.

If you have to pay full price for all the produce, as well as purchase the jars and needed supplies, you could be spending more than the cost of purchasing at the store. The advantage, however, is knowing the quality of produce you're putting in the jars. If the cost is the same as buying at the market, it's worth the extra time and work involved just to know you're getting fresh, quality food. Once you have accumulated the necessary canning supplies, check newspaper ads or online to see if you can get free or very inexpensive produce. If you are able to, the cost of canning is much less, plus you get the great quality and taste that comes from preserving fresh food.

Following is a list of items I preserve and how I prepare them. This will include procedures for canning as well as freezing foods. You will want to purchase a canning book to keep current on processing tips and times and to ensure safety of the food being preserved.

ZUCCHINI: Summer months are known for abundant crops of zucchini. While in season, we eat a lot of it because it's free, healthy, and doesn't preserve well. I use it sliced and sautéed in butter with onion, a little hot pepper, and seasoning. It works wonderful in stir fry and can be used fresh in green salads. Grated zucchini can be added to spaghetti sauce as healthy filler, and it's unlikely anyone will even notice it's there. Zucchini can also be grated and frozen to be used later in sauces or breads. I like to cube zucchini and freeze it to be used in vegetable soup during the winter.

BERRIES: I am blessed with my parents' infamous berry patch. I typically get as many as 18-20 gallons of fresh blackberries, which I wash and freeze by laying out on sheet pans. This keeps them from being all stuck together during freezing, making it easier to take out only what I need. These berries are great for milkshakes, smoothies, pies, and cheesecake topping. Frozen berries are also a nice, cool, and healthy snack on a hot summer day. Picking berries is back-breaking work but well worth it every time I open my freezer to bags of wonderful berries that only cost me the time and effort to pick.

CORN: If you live in a rural area where corn is grown, often you can find you-pick corn fields for really cheap. Picking corn is easy and takes very little time. Once you get the corn home, shuck it, blanch it for 2 minutes in hot boiling water, allow it to cool slightly, and then cut the kernels off the cob. An electric knife is essential for this job, making the work quick and easy. Put the desired amount in freezer bags and freeze. It's that simple, and you have fresh tasting corn all year long. An approximate way to figure how much corn you need is: three average-sized ears of corn equals one cup of kernels. That means you get about a quart of corn from a dozen ears. One more note. You may be tempted to allow your fresh-picked corn to sit for a day or two, but I can assure you time is of the essence. Corn that is allowed to sit loses flavor quickly.

GREEN BEANS: Beans should be *snapped* into bite sized pieces, washed, and then put in canning jars—pints or quarts depending on the size of your family. Add water and 1/2 teaspoon salt per pint of beans, and then process in a pressure cooker. See your canning book for processing time. I also like to freeze some beans to use in vegetable soups.

TOMATOES: In my opinion, tomatoes are the most important product I preserve each year. Thanks again to my parents and their prolific garden, combined with a few tomatoes from my garden, I am able to *can* 120 to 150

quarts each year. These tomatoes are a staple in my
kitchen because I make all my own Italian sauces, salsa,
chili, and soups from them. Wash the tomatoes and then
blanch them in boiling water for a few minutes, just long
enough to break the skin. Put the tomatoes in cold water
for a minute, and then peel and press into jars. This is a
job where a canning funnel comes in handy; press the
tomatoes together in the jar making sure there are no air
bubbles. Add a teaspoon of salt to each quart of tomatoes,
wipe the jar tops clean, and then put on hot lids and screw
rings on tight. Process quarts for 30 minutes in a
standard, boiling water-bath canner. Make sure to check
your canning book to confirm any processing time
changes. Tomatoes can also be frozen in freezer bags but I
prefer the taste of canned tomatoes better.

PEACHES AND PEARS: Fruit is the hardest thing for me
to can each year because it has to be perfectly ripened at
the time of canning. If it gets too ripe, it bruises and
doesn't can well. If fruit is too green, it won't have good
flavor and tends to be rubbery when canned. Also,
recommended types are Bartlett Pears and Elberta
Peaches. If the texture of a peach is stringy when you eat
it fresh, it will be that much more so when canned. Once
you get your fruit home, it just has to be washed, peeled,
and placed into jars. When the jar is full, pour hot syrup
(2 cups water to 1 cup sugar boiled to dissolve the sugar)
into the jar over the fruit, wipe the jar top, put on hot lids,
and screw the rings down tight. Process the jars in a
boiling water-bath for 20 minutes. Don't under-process
but over-processing will cause your fruit to get soft and
potentially mushy.

APPLE AND PEAR SAUCE: If you are an applesauce
lover, try making pear sauce. Wash, peel, trim, and cut
fruit in quarters. Cook until soft, usually only few
minutes; blend or mash the fruit to the desired texture,

add sugar to the desired sweetness, and then fill the jars. Wipe the jar tops, put on hot lids and the rings, and then process in a boiling water-bath for 20 minutes. It's a lot of work but oh, so tasty!

PEACH SYRUP: If you have peaches that don't appear to be good enough quality to can or they are over-ripe, use them to make fruit syrup or jam. It's a great way to use produce that is less than perfect. For making syrup, clean, peel, and puree the fruit; place 6 cups of the pureed fruit, 5 cups of sugar, and one cup of Karo Syrup into a pot; bring the mixture to a boil, and stir occasionally for approximately 4-5 minutes. Pour into jars, place on hot lids and the rings, and then process in boiling water-bath for 5 minutes. Your family will love homemade fruit syrup on their pancakes all year long; what a treat! Any type of fruit can be used, including plums and berries; if using berries, it's best to juice them and make syrup from the juice so it's not seedy.

PEACH JAM: For peach and all other jams, I recommend you follow the recipes on the pectin box; pectin is recommended for all jams and jellies. Every year I make peach, blackberry, strawberry, plum, and apricot jams and jellies, provided I can get the fruit. If you are looking for ways to give gifts at Christmas but not spend a lot of money, purchase jelly canning jars, make homemade jam and jelly, add a loaf of homemade bread, and then give as a gift for the holidays. It's inexpensive but such a wonderful gift, something that came from your hands and not the store!

GRAPE JUICE: You can make grape, plum, berry, apple, and other kinds of juice by purchasing a juicer and working hard. It's so nice to get the straight juice without all the extra sugar. Once you drink the pure stuff, you'll be spoiled. I recommend removing all stems and leaves before putting grapes or other fruit in the hopper; leaving on stems and leaves will cause your juice to be somewhat bitter. Most books say you can throw it all in, but from experience, I've found the extra time spent taking the grapes off the stems is well worth the effort based on the sweeter flavor. Often, people have grapes they never use, and you can get bushels free for the picking. Make certain you wait until after the first good freeze, usually around the middle of October, to harvest grapes. The freeze will *set* the sugar, giving you sweeter grapes.

CHILI BEANS: I can chili beans year round; they are a part of my weekly menu. You must have a pressure cooker canner to process them. Soak 3 cups of dry pinto beans overnight; drain off the water and add: 1 cup chopped onion (optional), 6 tablespoons of chili powder (one 12.4 oz. jar is 8 tablespoons), 2 tablespoons salt, ¼ teaspoon pepper, hot red pepper flakes (as desired), 1 pint canned tomatoes, and 7 ½ cups boiling water. Combine these ingredients, and boil for approximately 5 minutes. Fill jars with beans and liquid to within 1 inch from the jar top. Use your judgment and try to evenly disperse the beans and liquid; this will fill approximately 7-8 pints. Wipe the jar tops, place lids on, and then screw down the rings. Process the beans for one hour at 12 pounds pressure in a pressure cooker canner. Be sure to read instructions on processing with a pressure cooker or have someone that knows how to use them work with you the first couple times. They can be dangerous, but having someone help will set your mind at ease. I use chili beans to make chili, add to taco meat, and also heat and mash for refried beans. You can spread them on a tortilla, add cheese, and then enjoy an easy, inexpensive lunch. Once you try these, you won't want to be without them in your pantry.

CANNED TUNA AND SALMON: If you happen to live close to fresh seafood, canning tuna and salmon at home is a wonderful way to preserve fresh fish, especially if you get it for a great price. I highly recommend trimming all the dark spots off the meat before placing in jars. This will alleviate a strong fishy taste. I have done it both ways and my family definitely prefers the well trimmed meat. Pack the raw fish dry (without water) in the jars; you can add a teaspoon of cooking oil if preferred but not necessary. Canned fish processes for 100 minutes (1 hour and 40 minutes) in a pressure cooker canner.

There are many other things that can be canned such as jalapeno peppers (yum!). I suggest once you get the hang of basic canning, experiment with other things. If you get an abundance of some type of food that you don't want to spoil, chances are it can be preserved by canning. This is such a great way to help provide for your family, save money, and eat healthy; it just takes the determination and willingness to work hard. So, roll up your sleeves, get busy, and say with me, **I THINK I *CAN*, I THINK I *CAN* . . . and YES, you really can!**

Tag from Tim, a husband's perspective:

Often times canning season is time for me to roll up my sleeves and lend a helping hand. We freeze somewhere in the neighborhood of 30-40 quarts of corn annually. My job is to cut the corn off the cob. To do this I place a small coffee cup upside down in a large baking pan. Then I hold the ear of corn with the pointed end down and the ear at an angle resting on the cup. Using an electric knife, I cut the corn, making sure I don't cut too deep. I want to eat the corn, not the cob. Canning is back-breaking work. I appreciate Debbie's willingness to work hard preserving food in season, so we have an abundant supply of fruits and vegetables all year 'round. It is not only healthier for us but also a wise use of our resources, saving money on the food budget annually.

My Best Recipes, Menus, and Ideas

One of the keys to cooking meals your family loves is using recipes that are tried and true, practical, and easy to follow. If you can read a recipe, understand the instructions, and have the correct ingredients on hand, you'll likely succeed at cooking wonderful meals your family will enjoy eating. If you are not accustomed to cooking regularly but are working to make a change, there may be many ingredients you need to purchase and keep on hand in your pantry.

I keep a grocery list on my refrigerator at all times so when I run out or run low on an item, I can take a second to add it to the list. This keeps me from forgetting what's needed when I prepare to shop each month. The following is a list of staple items I purchase monthly at the store or keep on hand at all times:

- Salt
- Pepper
- Garlic (either fresh or granulated)
- Chili Powder
- Paprika
- Cream of Tarter
- Dry Mustard
- Creole/Cajon Seasoning

- Steak Seasoning
- Italian Seasoning
- Cumin
- Dried, crushed red peppers
- Chicken Base
- Beef Base
- Cream of Mushroom soup
- Corn Starch
- Flour
- White sugar
- Brown sugar
- Powdered sugar
- Cinnamon
- Dry Milk
- Cocoa
- Vanilla
- Cake/cookie sprinkles
- Coffee/Tea
- Cooking oil/Olive oil
- Rice
- Dry Beans (pinto, white, red or mixed)
- Potatoes
- Soda Crackers
- Peanut butter
- Honey
- Jam (homemade)
- Butter
- Tortillas
- Pasta

Side Note: There are some items I keep handy for emergency dinner plans which are inexpensive and can save you a lot of time in a pinch. Cake mixes, Jell-O, and Jiffy brand corn bread mix are some of them. If you can purchase cake mixes for under a dollar, the value is definitely there. Jell-O makes a great addition to a dinner, and most kids like it. If adding fruit to Jell-O, use the juice from the fruit as part of the added water. If you've never tried the Jiffy brand corn bread, it's a great balance between a *mealy* corn bread and a *cakey* corn bread. It costs less than fifty cents a box and will feed four to five people. It's cheap, easy, and tastes great!

Many of the recipes I have included in this chapter were selected for economic reasons because many of us are living on tight budgets and looking for ways to eat well, while making the dollar stretch. Also, this chapter of recipes is set up different than most recipe books but I trust you will find it an easy-to-follow guide, especially if you are using my menu planning suggestions. And, as stated in my last chapter, "If at first you don't succeed, try, try again!" So, here goes the cooking!

Mexican Meals

Tacos:

On taco night at my house I like to set out crunchy taco shells as well as corn and flour tortillas. We really like soft-crunchy tacos where you fix a crunchy shell and wrap it with a flour tortilla. If you've never tried it, you have to do it. It's yummy!

Beef – Fry up one pound of hamburger (with onion, pepper, and garlic if you like) and season with salt, pepper, crushed red pepper, chili powder, and granulated garlic and onion (if your kids don't like the chunks). Then add one pint of your home-canned chili beans or a can from the store. If it is a little extra saucy, you can simmer it for a few minutes to thicken.

Chicken – I purchase large bags of individually frozen boneless, skinless chicken breast from the store. Take out three large breasts, thaw, then cut in small pieces, and fry up in butter. When cooked, add seasoning as you would with beef or even season with a little salsa. You can also boil the breast until extra tender then shred with a fork and add the seasoning.

Pork – Cook a small pork roast in the crock pot or boil it on the stove until well cooked and tender. Drain the water, shred with a fork, and then add your favorite seasonings and/or salsa.

Note: When seasoning food, add a little at a time, and then taste. This will keep you from adding too much of one thing. Also, most canned items have plenty of salt in them; therefore, go light on the salt when using purchased canned items.

Topping suggestions – Lettuce, tomato, onion, olives, avocado, sour cream, salsa, and shredded cheese (cheddar and/or Monterey jack)

Burritos:

Using flour tortillas, spread with meat (you can use the same meat from tacos in your burritos), cheese, and any other toppings you like, wrap up, and eat. Spread refried beans on flour tortillas, add cheese, and you have a fast, easy lunch. I prefer my home-canned chili beans heated up and mashed. Beans will be a little runny at first but will thicken as you continue to mash.

Fried Burritos – Put meat or beans and cheese in a flour tortilla, wrap up, and fry in a pan with butter. Eat with sour cream and salsa on top!

Enchiladas:

Beef - Again, the same meat can be used as in tacos and burritos but use corn tortillas instead of flour. Make a paste with chili powder and water; dip corn tortilla on both sides and fry in Canola Oil turning once just long enough to stick paste to tortilla. Put meat and cheese in the tortilla, roll, and lay in pan. When the pan is full, pour homemade salsa or enchilada sauce over the top and bake at 350 degrees for approximately 20-30 minutes. Top with sour cream and salsa.

Chicken – Boil and chop 4 large boneless, skinless chicken breasts. Add 2 cans cream of chicken soup (or make one batch from white sauce recipe), 1 pint sour cream, 1 large can diced chilies, and 1/2 cup chicken broth. Mix all together. Spread a thin layer in the bottom of 9 X 13-inch pan; then layer 4 corn tortillas, 1/3 of the chicken mixture and cheddar cheese; repeat for 3 layers. Bake at 350 degrees for approximately 45 minutes. Top with sour cream and salsa.

Taco Salads:

Use the same beef, pork, chicken, or beans. Put tortilla chips in bowl; top with meat, cheese, and salsa. Then add salad and dressing...ranch is the best dressing for taco salads.

Spanish Rice:

Melt 2 tablespoons of butter in a small pot. Add 2 cups of rice, and lightly brown on the stove, stirring occasionally. Add approximately 2/3 cup salsa, salt and pepper, and stir. Complete by adding 4 cups of water, bring to a boil, stir again, then put on a tight lid, and turn burner to low. Allow to simmer for 24 minutes without lifting the lid on the pan. Your rice should be perfectly cooked! Stir lightly with fork and eat.

Note: You can take leftover rice and meat or beans, mix together in a baking dish, sprinkle with cheese and heat thoroughly. It can be eaten on a tortilla or as a casserole with sour cream and salsa. I also like to add corn if there happens to be any leftover in my fridge from a previous meal. This makes a quick, yummy lunch or dinner the next day.

Chili Verde:

In a large pot, boil 1 small pork roast with salt, pepper, and chicken base until very tender, and then remove the meat from the pot. (Pork can be substituted with chicken if preferred.) Using the same pot and broth from the meat, add 1 medium diced onion, 3 chopped celery stalks, 1 diced jalapeno pepper, crushed red pepper, salt, black pepper (to taste), 1 pint of crushed or home-canned tomatoes, and 1 can cream of mushroom soup. Bring to a boil, and then reduce the heat to a simmer until all vegetables are tender. Add the chopped or shredded pork back into the pan and mix. Lightly thicken with 1/4 cup cornstarch and 2-3 tablespoons of water. (Note: Use cold water with cornstarch.) Serve Chili Verde over cooked rice, wrapped in a flour tortilla, or with a tortilla on the side and add sour cream and salsa on top.

Variation: chili beans can be added to the mix and you have Chalupas!

Rice: To cook the perfect rice, bring 4 cups of water in a pot to a boil; add 2 cups of rice, a pinch of salt, then stir and put on lid; turn the burner to a low setting, and let the rice simmer for 24 minutes without lifting the lid on the pot. When done, stir and serve.

Salsa: Salsa can be made many ways for many different tastes. In the summer when tomatoes are in the garden, green and red tomatoes can be chopped fresh and added to chopped onion, green and red peppers, hot peppers, garlic, chili powder, salt and pepper. If you have children that do not like the chunky salsas, put all these ingredients in a blender and blend to desired consistency. You can eat this salsa fresh, or put it on the stove and simmer for 30 minutes. Fresh salsa has a bolder flavor whereas cooking the salsa gives a milder taste.

To make salsa when I no longer have fresh garden tomatoes, combine 1 quart of home-canned tomatoes with onion, peppers (hot, mild, and crushed red), garlic, chili powder, salt, and black pepper in the blender. Blend until smooth then heat on the stove.

Other thoughts on Mexican Meals: Warming tortillas can be done in different ways; crunchy taco shells can be heated in the microwave; flour tortillas can also be heated in the microwave, but if you freeze tortillas like I do, it's best to make sure they are thawed completely before heating. Another way to heat flour and corn tortillas is on a grill. Just throw on the grill and turn to other side when heated. This is a healthier alternative than frying corn tortillas in oil.

If you are throwing a party, a Mexican Fiesta is a great way to go. You can cook a variety of dishes yet use the same meat and ingredients for most of them. It's easy, economical, and really yummy!

Italian Meals

Marinara Red Sauce:

In a blender, combine 1 quart canned tomatoes, 1/4 small onion, 1/4 large green pepper, 1-2 garlic cloves (or granulated garlic if preferred), 2 tablespoons (or to taste) mixed dry Italian seasonings, 1 teaspoon sugar, and salt and black pepper (to taste). Blend until smooth. If you prefer chunky sauce, chop additional onion, pepper, garlic, and fresh tomato, and add them to the sauce after blending. Add 1/2 to 1 can of cream of mushroom soup. (I use 1 can for a double batch.) Simmer on low for 1-2 hours or in a crock pot for the day. This recipe can be easily doubled for larger families or groups. I always double it for my family, and we have leftovers for another meal.

Alfredo Sauce:

Place 1 cube of butter in a microwavable bowl and melt in a microwave oven; with wire whisk, mix in 6 tablespoons flour, then some salt, pepper, granulated garlic, and 1/2 teaspoon dry mustard. Slowly whip in 2 cups cream and 2 cups whole milk. Heat in the microwave oven, stirring every 2 minutes until the sauce is thickened (approximately 9 minutes). This amount will feed 8-10 people and is the amount I use for my family. You can divide the recipe in half for smaller servings.

Spaghetti:

Fry 1 to 1 1/2 pounds of ground beef and add to the Marinara Sauce. Cook 1 package of spaghetti noodles, and serve with fresh or grated parmesan cheese. An old family tradition is to eat spaghetti and sauce with mustard on top. Try it, you may be surprised!

Lasagna:

Prepare 1 batch of Marinara Sauce. Fry 1 pound of ground beef. Cook 9 lasagna noodles in a large pot until soft enough to poke with fork but still a little chewy. (Adding a tablespoon of olive or canola oil to the water will help keep noodles from sticking together.) Spray the bottom of a 9x13 or 11x14 inch pan. (Use the same amount of noodles for both sizes of pans) Spread a thin layer of sauce in bottom of pan, and then make three complete layers of: noodles, sauce, meat, parmesan cheese, and mozzarella cheese. (Each layer uses 3 noodles.) Bake at 375 degrees for 45 minutes or until bubbly.

Homemade Pizza:

Crust – Dissolve 2 tablespoons yeast, 2 cups warm water, and 1 tablespoon sugar or honey in a glass bowl. In a separate bowl or heavy duty mixer, combine 2 cups flour, 2 teaspoons salt, 4 tablespoons olive oil, and 4 crushed garlic cloves. Add the water/yeast mixture to the dry ingredients and mix well; gradually add in 3-4 more cups of flour and knead in machine for 8-10 minutes. If kneading by hand, mix in as much flour as possible with mixer then continue kneading by hand for 10 – 12 minutes, adding flour as needed. Allow rising until double (approximately 30 minutes); then punch the dough down and divide in half. Each half will do one sheet pan of pizza.

While dough is rising, mix up one batch of Marinara Sauce and prepare toppings: cooked ground beef seasoned with Italian seasonings, Italian sausage, Canadian bacon, pepperoni, fresh crispy bacon (one of my personal favorite toppings), onion, green pepper, mushrooms, and anything else you like on your pizza.

If available, a pizza roller works great for rolling out dough on sheet pans. Once rolled out, allow the dough to rise approximately 10 minutes before adding toppings. Bake at 400 degrees for 15-20 minutes.

Tip: I have discovered pre-shredded mozzarella cheese is as economical as purchasing it in a block. If this is the case for you, save yourself extra work and purchase it already shredded. Also, seasoned ground beef is an inexpensive meat to top your pizza with, and one small package of sliced pepperoni goes a long way. Homemade pizza is a fun meal to prepare and serve for a child's birthday party.

Chicken Alfredo:

Cube 2-3 large chicken breasts while melting 1/2 cube butter in a large skillet. Sauté the chicken in the butter while mixing up a batch of Alfredo sauce without cooking it. Cook fettuccini noodles (or other pasta such as penne or bowtie) until tender. When chicken is completely cooked, add sauce, and cook stirring constantly until thickened. Serve by ladling sauce with chicken over the pasta; top with parmesan cheese.

Parmesan Chicken:

Thaw chicken breast according to the number of servings you need. In bowl, beat 2 eggs with 1/2 cup milk. In a separate bowl, combine 1 cup Italian-seasoned bread crumbs (You can used crushed soda crackers seasoned up with Italian seasonings if you don't have bread crumbs.), 1/3 cup flour, 1/3 cup grated parmesan cheese, salt, pepper, and garlic. Dip chicken in the egg mixture, roll in the crumbs, and place on a greased baking dish. Sprinkle with fresh grated parmesan cheese and drizzle with melted butter. Bake at 375 degrees for approximately 30 minutes or until done. Serve chicken breast with your choice of pasta and marinara sauce.

Other thoughts on Italian Meals: I serve most Italian dishes with home-made bread and fresh green salad. All my salads are made with Romaine lettuce as Romaine is high in protein and great tasting, not bitter.

Soups

My family loves soup! I can think of nothing better on a cold fall or winter day than hot soup with homemade bread. I have learned to make soup by experimenting; therefore, I typically don't use recipes for them. For your benefit, I wrote out recipes, guessing portions on certain items. You will want to adjust seasonings to fit your family's preference. Once you start making soups, you will find them to be not only tasty but really fun to make!

Once a year my husband and I do a membership meeting at our home for new families desiring to join our church's membership. For this meeting, I always make a variety of soups, served with a couple different types of bread, salad, and a beverage. It's a light meal but I get rave reviews from everyone who attends. Soup isn't just for an easy meal night, it's for guests too! Therefore, make a big pot of soup and invite friends over for a night of fellowship; everyone will be glad you did!

Cream Base for Cream Soups:

This cream base is the same sauce I use for Alfredo except you may want to use all milk instead of part cream and cut the recipe in half. Using all milk is more economical and less fattening but not quite as rich and creamy.

Cream Base: Melt 1/2 cube (1/4 cup) of butter in microwaveable bowl. With wire whisk, mix in 3 tablespoons of flour, salt, pepper, garlic (powdered, granulated, or minced), and dry mustard. Gradually mix in 2 cups of milk. Microwave for approximately 8 minutes, stirring with wire whisk every 2 minutes until thickened.

Note: If needing a chicken cream base, simply add approximately 2 teaspoons of chicken base to the cream base recipe before cooking.

Potato Soup:

Cube 10 small to medium sized potatoes and place in a large pot, covered with water. Salt and pepper, then cook on the stove top until potatoes are tender. Stir in 1 recipe of cream sauce, mixing well. You may want to add a little chicken base for extra flavor. Serve soup topped with hot, crumbled, and crispy bacon, chives, and cheddar cheese.

Cheddar Cheese Soup:

Combine 3 cubed potatoes and 1 shredded carrot in a large pot. Cover with water then add chicken base, salt, and pepper; cook till potatoes are tender. Add 1 batch of cream base, stirring well then 1-2 cups shredded cheddar cheese and stir till melted.

Cream of Chicken Soup:

Bring to boil and simmer 2-3 chicken breasts till well cooked and tender; remove meat from pan and finely chop or shred. Add chicken base, salt, and pepper to the water. Stir in 1 batch of cream base then add the chicken back into the pot; stir and serve.

Variations:

With a little imagination, you can make all kinds of cream soups using the cream base. Experiment with celery, mushroom, or even tomato cream soup. I sometimes add green peas to my cream soups for extra color! Don't be afraid to experiment!

Bean Soup:

Cover 3 cups of mixed dried beans with water and soak overnight. Drain water and place the beans in a crock pot with 1 pint of canned tomatoes, 1 small onion, 1 small green pepper, 2 garlic cloves, and seasonings. If you prefer a spicier soup, add chili powder and hot pepper with 1 pound of cooked ground beef. If you like Italian soup, add Italian seasonings and 1 pound cooked Italian sausage. Salt, pepper, and ham can be added for a mild soup. Cover with boiling water and cook on low for approximately 10 hours. (You may also add pre-cooked sea-shell pasta to

Italian soup at end of cooking time.) Serve with fresh French bread or Jiffy corn bread.

White Chili:

Boil 3 chicken breast with onion, chicken base, salt, and black pepper until chicken is tender. Remove chicken from the pan and add 2 quarts of canned white navy beans. Heat on med-low temperature, and while the beans are heating, cube the chicken. Add the chicken back in and heat thoroughly. Season to taste.

Beef Chili:

Fry 1 1/2 - 2 pounds of ground beef with 1 small onion and 1 green, yellow, or red pepper in large pot. Add 1 quart of canned tomatoes, 3 quarts chili beans, crushed red pepper, garlic, salt, and pepper. Adding canned tomatoes will give you a thinner chili; blending the tomatoes before adding will make it slightly thicker. For a thick chili, leave out tomatoes or use only one pint. Thoroughly heat and serve with Fritos, sour cream, and cheese on top.

Taco Salads: Put tortilla chips in bottom of bowl and cover with chili; sprinkle with cheddar cheese, salsa, and sour cream. Spread lettuce on top, and then eat with ranch dressing. This is an easy way to make taco salads and use leftover chili.

Chili Enchiladas: Roll a corn tortilla with shredded cheddar or pepper jack cheese and salsa; place in baking dish. Pour chili over the top, sprinkle with a little extra cheese, and bake at 375 degrees until hot and bubbly. Serve with sour cream, chips, and salsa.

Taco Soup:

Chicken: Start with 3 chicken breasts boiled with chicken base, onion, green pepper, and garlic until tender. Cube

or shred chicken. Add corn, chili beans, crushed red
pepper, salt, and black pepper.

Ground Beef: Fry 1 1/2 pounds meat with onion and
pepper in large pan until thoroughly cooked. Add 1 quart
of chili beans, 1-2 cups beef broth, corn, hot pepper, and
other preferred seasonings. Additional water and
seasonings can be added for a thinner consistency; less for
a thicker soup.

Beef Stew:

Cube 1-2 pounds round steak. In a large pot, fry meat in
cooking oil, and then cover well in beef broth. Add salt,
pepper, and garlic; simmer until meat is tender. Add 4
medium potatoes, 2 sliced carrots, 2 celery sticks, and 1
small onion. Add additional water as needed, cooking
until all vegetables are soft. Thicken slightly with either
cornstarch or flour and water. (When using flour and
water, blend in blender to minimize lumps.) Season to
taste.

Note: You can make beef stew using leftover roast beef
and gravy. Combine in a large pot, add extra beef broth
and the desired vegetables, and cook until vegetables are
tender.

Minestrone Soup:

In large pot, place 2 cubed medium-sized potatoes, 2
peeled and chopped or sliced carrots, 1 small onion, 1 cup
frozen green beans, 1 cup frozen corn, 1 pint canned
tomatoes, and 1 quart canned chili beans. Cover with
water and simmer until tender. Season with chili powder,
salt, pepper, and garlic. Make different varieties by adding
cooked ground beef or sausage and pasta.

Hearty Vegetable Beef Soup:

In a large pot, combine all your favorite vegetables (carrots, peas, beans, corn, squash, onions, peppers, potatoes). Keep in mind, a handful of each veggie will make a big pot. Add 1 quart canned tomatoes, salt, and pepper, and then cover with water and cook until tender. While cooking, fry 1 pound of ground beef. When the vegetables are done, add the meat and season to taste.

Chicken Noodle Soup:

Boil 3 large chicken breasts in large pot. Remove meat then add chicken base, 1/2 chopped small onion, 1/2 cup peas, and 1/2 cup chopped carrot to broth. Cook for 10 minutes, and then add 2 cups egg noodles. While the noodles are cooking, cut meat and return it to the pot. Season to taste. Broth may be thickened if preferred (1/2 cup flour blended with 1/2 cup water; poured slowly into the pot through a strainer, stirring constantly to desired thickness).

Chicken and Dumplings:

Combine 3 large chicken breasts, 1 onion, 2 stalks celery cut in small cubes, chicken base, salt, pepper, garlic, and celery salt in large pot. Cover with water and cook until chicken is tender, approximately 1 – 1 1/2 hours. Remove chicken and cut into bite sized pieces. Return chicken to pot with 1/2 cup peas and reheat to boiling. Blend 1/2 cup flour, 1/2 cup water, garlic, salt, and pepper; gradually add the flour to the chicken pot, stirring constantly to thicken. Bring back to boiling point.

Dumplings are made by mixing 1 1/2 cups flour, 1 teaspoon dry parsley flakes, 2 teaspoons baking powder, and 1/2 teaspoon salt in bowl. Combine 2/3 cup milk, 2 tablespoons oil, and 1 beaten egg together. Add milk mixture to dry ingredients and stir with a fork until ingredients are mixed and moistened.

Drop dumplings, one spoonful at a time, onto the top of simmering chicken pot. Sprinkle with salt and pepper, cover tightly with lid, and boil gently for 15-20 minutes or until dumplings look fluffy and dry. Serve in bowls.

Homemade Chicken and Noodles:

In large pot, cook 3 large chicken breasts with chicken base, salt, and pepper until tender. While chicken is cooking, prepare noodles. Beat 5 large eggs and 1 tablespoon milk together in a bowl. Add, garlic, salt, and pepper. Gradually add in enough flour to form dough. Roll out thin on well floured table; it may be easier to roll out dough in sections. Slice dough in narrow strips forming noodles. Lay cut noodles in large, well floured sheet pans to dry and sprinkle any remaining flour left on table on top of noodles. When chicken is done, remove from pan and add noodles to broth. Add all flour on the pan with noodles. This will thicken the broth as the noodles cook. Chop or shred chicken then add back in and continue to cook until noodles are done. Add additional salt and pepper to taste.

Leftovers Soup:

Any time you have leftover meats, sauces, gravy, veggies, potatoes, and/or rice, you have the potential of a quick, yummy soup. Throw the ingredients into a pot with broth or canned tomatoes and you have a quick, hot meal! Leftover spaghetti sauce is a great seasoning and addition to Italian, beef, or vegetable soups; leftover chicken Alfredo can be added to boiled potatoes to make a wonderful potato soup with chicken. Leftovers can also be put in a crock pot to heat during the day, and you have dinner waiting for you when you're ready!

Serve soup with breads and salads. This makes a perfect meal on a cold, snowy or rainy day.

BBQ Meals

Grilled Chicken:

Place 8 boneless chicken breast in a deep bowl. Add half of a sliced onion and 1 sliced green pepper on top of chicken. Mix together 1/2 cup soy sauce, 1/2 cup cooking oil, 1/4 cup catsup, 2 tablespoons vinegar, 1/2 teaspoon black pepper, 1/2 teaspoon salt, and 1/2 teaspoon granulated garlic. Pour over the chicken and sprinkle with a little crushed red pepper (optional). Marinate for 24 hours, and then cook on a hot gas grill or briquettes. This is the best, no-fail grilled chicken recipe anywhere. Serve it to your guests and they will rave about your cooking, especially if you serve cheesy potatoes with it!

Serving Suggestions: Serve with cheesy potatoes, corn and green salad.

Cheesy Potatoes: Peel and cube (approximately 1/2-inch cubes) 8 cups potatoes; cook in boiling water until tender but not mushy. Drain off all water. Gently mix in 2 tablespoons finely chopped chives and 2 teaspoons salt. While potatoes are cooking, melt 1 cube of butter; then add 1 can cream of mushroom soup, 16 ounces (1 pint) of sour cream and 3 1/2 cups grated cheddar cheese. Pour over potatoes, and then sprinkle 1/2 cup grated cheddar cheese and paprika on top. Cover and bake at 350 degrees for 45 minutes.

Grilled Steaks:

If marinated correctly, even a cheap cut of steak can be exceptionally tasty! Lay steaks out on a sheet pan and marinate both sides by generously sprinkling with lemon juice and Worcestershire sauce. Then sprinkle with a steak seasoning and/or salt, pepper, and garlic. For cheaper cuts of meat that tend to be tough, you can marinate up to 24 hours; for more tender cuts, 8 – 10 hours is usually plenty of time. Place on hot grill and cook as desired.

Serving Suggestions: Serve with baked or oven fried potatoes, vegetables, bread, and green salad. You can offer steak or BBQ sauce; however, a well marinated steak doesn't need extra sauces; the flavor will be great without it.

Baked Potatoes: Foil wrap the desired number of potatoes, or coat the potatoes with cooking oil. Bake in a 400-degree oven for 45 minutes to 1 hour or until soft enough to press between thumb and index finger. Serve with toppings such as butter, sour cream, salt, pepper, crispy bacon, chives, and/or ranch dressing.

Oven Fried Potatoes: Peel and slice the desired number of potatoes, placing them on a baking sheet. Thinly slice 1 small onion and layer over the top of the potatoes. Pour melted butter over top, and then sprinkle with salt, pepper, garlic, Creole seasoning, paprika, and/or chives. Bake at 400 degrees for approximately 45 minutes or until tender and/or crispy.

Grilled Hamburgers and Hotdogs:

Season your hamburger with Worcestershire sauce, salt, pepper, garlic, and a little BBQ sauce. If you like spicy food, sprinkle a little crushed red pepper in your meat as well. Mix with your hands, and then form patties. I prefer thin patties to ensure they cook thoroughly and quickly. Grill on a hot surface until desired doneness. Hot dogs can be cooked just until heated through or burned on the grill for extra flavor. Serve on a bun with your favorite condiments such as cheese, lettuce, tomato, onion, pickles, mustard, mayonnaise, catsup, BBQ sauce, and relish.

Serving Suggestions: So many side dishes can be added to your grilled burgers and hotdogs: french fries, potato salad, macaroni salad, Jell-o, baked beans, potato chips, fruit salad, and melons just to name a few.

Potato and Macaroni Salads: I make both of these salads with the same basic dressing. Start by cooking macaroni until tender (don't overcook) and/or boil potatoes whole with peel on until tender enough to poke with a fork. Cool completely. Boil eggs on the stove by placing 8-12 eggs in a pot, cover with water, add salt, and boil 12 minutes. Remove from heat and let stand approximately 30 minutes. Drain and peel. For potatoes, peel and cube in the desired size; place in large bowl. Pour 1/4 - 1/3 cup pickle juice from a jar of dill pickles over the macaroni or potatoes. Let stand while mixing 2 cups mayo, 1/4 cup mustard (adjust mustard to taste), salt, pepper, garlic, and 1 tablespoon pickle juice. Chop desired number of eggs and add to potatoes or pasta. Pour sauce over potatoes or macaroni and eggs. Mix thoroughly and adjust seasoning to taste.

BBQ Ribs:

Boil ribs in a large pot until just done. Season meat with salt, pepper, garlic, and/or other desired spices. Coat ribs with desired BBQ sauce. (Any kind works, so use your favorite.) Let the ribs stand for a couple hours, and then brown on hot grill until both sides are nicely marked from the grill bars and well-flavored from the grill smoke. Easy yet tasty!

Variation: Place ribs on grill and cook until brown. Salt and pepper, cut to size and put into a crock pot with sliced onion; cover with BBQ Sauce and cook on high for approximately 4 hours or until meat is tender.

Barbeque Sauce: Combine 1/3 cup catsup, 2 tablespoons vinegar, 1/3 cup water, 1 tablespoon brown sugar, 1 tablespoon Worcestershire sauce, and 1/4 teaspoon garlic salt. Mix well and pour over meat.

Serving Suggestions: Oven-fried potato wedges (recipe can be found with meatloaf) and corn on the cob are great additions to BBQ Ribs.

Grilled Halibut:

Because fish tends to fall apart when cooked on the grill, you can do one of three things. Place foil on the grill (use a heavy duty foil to keep it from tearing) under the fish, wrap the fish in foil before placing it on the grill, or place the fish in a cast-iron skillet covered with foil then set on grill to cook. Any way you choose, sprinkle the fish with lemon juice and lightly coat with salt or Creole seasoning, garlic, and black pepper. Add a little butter by placing small pieces on top. Cook on the grill until completely done. Serve hot and steamy. (Of course, if you don't have a grill, place in the oven and bake.)

Serving Suggestions: Serve with mixed vegetables or squash, rice pilaf, green salad, and bread.

Rice Pilaf: Melt 3 tablespoons of butter in sauce pot. Sauté 1/2 cup shredded carrots, 2 tablespoons finely chopped onion, and 1/4 cup finely chopped celery until tender. Add 2 cups rice and stir to coat with butter and vegetables, pour 4 cups chicken broth over rice, bring to a boil, stir, turn burner down to low, place lid tightly on pan, and then let simmer for 24 minutes.

Crock Pot Meals

Roast Beef:

Place a 3-4 pound roast in a Dutch oven or crock pot. Slice onion over the top, and add salt and pepper. Spread 1 can cream of mushroom soup over the roast, and pour 1 1/2 cups beef broth with 2 teaspoons of Worcestershire Sauce mixed in over the top. Cook on high for 6 hours in a crock pot or in the oven at 350 degrees for approximately 3-4 hours or until tender.

Serving Suggestions: Serve with mashed potatoes and gravy, green beans, and green salad.

Gravy: Pour liquid from meat into a sauce pot; bring to boil and thicken to desired consistency with cornstarch and cold water mix. Season to taste.

Mashed Potatoes: Peel and cube desired amount of potatoes; place in pot and cover with water. (If using red potatoes, no need to peel.) Cook until tender then drain. Using hand mixer, whip potatoes with butter, sour cream, and salt (portions based on amount of potatoes used). Add a few teaspoons of butter on top to melt and sprinkle with pepper.

Ham:

Place ham in crock pot; mix up 1/2 cup honey and 1 tablespoon mustard in a cup. Pour over ham, add 1 cup of water to bottom of pot, and mill some fresh ground black pepper on top. Cover and cook on high for approximately 6 hours.

Serving Suggestions: Serve with Cheesy Potatoes (recipe with grilled chicken), green beans, and green salad or fruit.

Beans and Ham:

Soak navy or pinto beans in pot over night. Drain, rinse, and place the beans in crock pot. Add 1/2 cup chopped onion, salt, pepper, and leftover ham with the bone into the pot. Cover completely with boiling water and cook on high for 10 hours.

Serving Suggestions: Serve with Tabasco sauce and corn bread with butter and honey.

Barbeque Chicken:

Place chicken thighs and/or legs in the crock pot; slice onion and green pepper and lay on chicken. Salt and pepper then cover with favorite BBQ sauce. Cook on high 5-6 hours or low for up to 10 hours until done.

Serving Suggestions: If you cook until tender, you can spoon chicken out with sauce and serve over steamed rice. Serve with vegetable and green salad.

Crockpot Steak:

Place 1 to 2 large round steaks cut in quarters in crock pot; add sliced onion, sweet red and yellow peppers, and quartered mushrooms to the pot. Pour 2 cups beef broth and 1 can cream of mushroom soup over top. Cook 5 hours on high or all day on low. Pour broth into a pot and thicken with corn starch and water for gravy. Place meat and gravy together in a bowl to serve.

Serving Suggestions: Serve over cooked rice, (see directions for making perfect rice in the Mexican recipes for Chili Verde), add green beans, green salad and bread.

Buckaroo Beans:

Soak 3 cups of pinto beans overnight. Drain, rinse, and place in a crock pot. Add 1 cup chopped onion, 2 cloves minced garlic, 1 pint (2 cups) canned tomatoes, 1 small chopped pepper, 1 tablespoon chili powder, 2 tablespoons brown sugar, 1 teaspoon dry mustard, 1/2 teaspoon cumin, salt, and pepper. Cover with boiling water and let cook on high all day until the beans are really tender. You can add 1/2 pound bacon, ham, or ground beef if desired.

Serving Suggestions: Serve over cooked rice with sour cream and corn bread. Add a green salad and you have an inexpensive yet really hearty meal.

Additional Helps: Crock pot meals are perfect for working moms, Sunday dinners, or exceptionally busy days. They are easy to prepare and cook by themselves allowing you freedom to do other things. Also, I like to put frozen meat in the crock pot with all the other ingredients on Saturday night, so Sunday morning, I just plug it in, and let it cook while we are at church. I finish up side dishes which are prepped or prepared the night before, also, and we are ready to eat a great meal in a short amount of time. Crock pots can become a mom's best friend on busy days!

Favorite American Meals

Meatloaf:

Combine 2 pounds diet lean or extra lean ground beef, 3 large eggs, 16 crushed soda cracker or equivalent of 4 slices of bread made into crumbs, 1/2 cup finely chopped onion (this can be left out for picky eaters), 2 teaspoons dry pepper flakes (optional), 1 tablespoon salt, black pepper, and 1/2 teaspoon thyme.

In a separate bowl, mix 1 cup catsup, 1/4 cup brown sugar, 1 tablespoon white vinegar, 2 teaspoons dry mustard, and 2 teaspoons regular mustard. Reserve 1/2 cup of the sauce and add rest the rest to the meat mixture.

Mix the sauce and meat mixture thoroughly together with your hands, and then lightly pack in a 2-quart casserole dish or 9-inch square pan. Spread with reserved sauce, and bake at 350 degrees for 1 hour. Let stand for 10 minutes and slice.

Serving Suggestions: Serve with potato wedges, cooked vegetables, and green salad.

Potato Wedges: Peel potatoes, cut into wedges, and place on a baking sheet. Drizzle with butter, salt, pepper, garlic, paprika, and chives. Bake at 400 degrees for approximately 45 minutes or until desired doneness. I prefer cooking until a little crispy on top or bottom.

Green Beans: Adding a teaspoon of bacon grease, slices of onion quartered, salt, and pepper to your green beans will add great flavor. You can add a small amount of butter and mushrooms, too, if desired. I prefer canned beans but frozen will work (frozen beans will need to cook longer).

Amazing Mac & Cheese:

Cook 2 cups of macaroni until just tender; drain thoroughly. While pasta is cooking, prepare the following ingredients: 1 teaspoon of butter, 1 beaten egg, 1 teaspoon each of salt and dry mustard mixed with 1 tablespoon hot water, 1 cup milk, and 3-4 cups shredded sharp cheddar cheese. After draining the macaroni, stir in butter and egg until the butter is melted. Combine the salt and dry mustard mix with the milk and pour into the macaroni. Finally, stir in the cheese, reserving enough to sprinkle a little on top. Bake at 350 degrees for approximately 45 minutes or until set up (not runny) and top is crusty. If you prefer a soft moist top, cover with foil before baking.

Serving Suggestions: Serve with a canned fruit like applesauce or peaches, green salad, and bread. Your family will never eat boxed Mac & Cheese again!

Meatballs:

Porcupine Meatballs: Mix 1 pound ground beef, 1/2 cup minced or finely chopped onion, 1/2 cup uncooked rice, and salt and pepper. Make 1-inch balls and place in a greased casserole dish. Mix up 1 batch of cream base (from soup section) and blend 1/2 celery stalk with milk before adding to the sauce. Pour cooked sauce over meatballs and bake at 350 degrees for 1 hour.

Barbeque Meatballs: Mix 1 pound ground beef, 1 egg, 1 cup quick oats, 1/2 cup minced or finely chopped onion, 1/2 cup milk or cream, salt, and pepper together in a large bowl. Roll the meat mixture into 1-inch sized balls and place single-layered in a greased casserole dish. Mix 1 1/2 cups catsup, 1 cup brown sugar, 1 tablespoon mustard, and 1/2 teaspoon salt together; pour the sauce over meatballs and bake at 350 degrees for 1 hour. Serve meatballs and sauce over rice.

Serving Suggestions: Serve with corn, green salad or fruit, and bread.

Country Fried Steak:

Dip desired number of cube steaks in 2 beaten eggs with a little milk. Roll in a mixture of bread crumbs, flour, salt, and pepper. Fry in bacon grease on the stove over medium heat or bake in the oven at 375 degrees for approximately 40 minutes, until done.

Cream Gravy: Use all drippings from cooking steak (approximately 2 tablespoons). Blend 2 cups whole milk, 3 tablespoons flour, 1 teaspoon salt, and 1/4 teaspoon pepper. Add to hot pan drippings and cook, stirring constantly, until gravy thickens; season to taste with salt and pepper. This will serve approximately 4 people. If serving larger groups, you may want to double this recipe.

Serving Suggestions: Serve steak with oven fried potatoes (recipe with the grilled steak recipe), gravy, corn, and green salad.

Jambolaya:

Fry 1 1/2 pounds ground beef with chopped onion; add 1 quart tomatoes, 1 teaspoon chili powder, 1/4 teaspoon cumin, salt and pepper; simmer on medium-low for 30 minutes, and then stir in 2 cups cooked rice. Continue cooking for 20 more minutes. Sprinkle with cheese allowing the cheese to melt.

Serving Suggestions: Serve with corn, green salad, and corn bread.

Pepper Steak:

Sauté 2 pounds of cubed round steak in 1 cube of butter. Add 3 cups beef stock, 2 tablespoons soy sauce, 1/2 teaspoon garlic salt, salt, and pepper. Cover the pan, and simmer for 1 1/2 - 2 hours or until meat is fork-tender, adding extra water as needed. Add 2 green peppers cut into strips, 1 thinly sliced onion, and 5 stalks chopped celery. Simmer for 10 minutes, and then thicken with 2 tablespoons of corn starch in water.

Serving Suggestions: Serve over cooked rice with soy sauce and fresh green salad.

Beef Stroganoff:

In large pan, fry 2 pounds of cubed round steak in 6 tablespoons butter. Sprinkle with salt and pepper, and then add 1/2 cup chopped onion and 2 cups beef stock (2 cubes bullion or 2 teaspoon of beef paste to 2 cups hot water). Simmer for approximately 1 1/2 hours, adding extra water as needed. Add one 8 ounce can mushrooms drained, 3 tablespoons tomato paste, and 1 tablespoon Worcestershire sauce. Mix well then add 1 cup sour cream. Stir and heat to serving temperature.

Serving Suggestions: Serve over cooked rice with vegetable and green salad.

Dessert Ideas

Growing up, both Tim and I were accustomed to desserts every evening after dinner. If you're like us, you know it's a hard habit to break. Depending on dietary needs, I want to give you some recipes and suggestions for serving something sweet, while keeping portions minimal. Also, I have included some healthy alternatives for those looking to control calories and watch the fat.

Fruit Desserts:

Fruit and Yogurt: Mixing chopped fresh fruit with flavored yogurt makes a healthy, sweet snack. Also, odd as it may sound, a pear half with a little mayo and grated cheddar cheese is very yummy if you've never tried it.

Rice Delight: Mix 2 cups plain cooked rice with 1 pint chopped canned peaches and an 8 ounce tub of cool whip. Sweet but low in fat.

Fresh Peaches: Sliced fresh peaches, served with a little cream or whole milk and sprinkled with sugar is yummy when peaches are in season.

Baked Apples: Core and peel apples; stuff with butter, brown sugar, and cinnamon. Bake at 350 degrees for 30 – 45 minutes until the butter and brown sugar melt and the apple is tender.

Cooked Apples: Peel and slice fresh apples, cover with water, and cook until tender. Drain excess water, and then add a little butter, sugar (white or brown), and cinnamon. Serve warm.

Peach Cobbler: Place 4 cups sliced, canned peaches into a buttered, 8-inch square pan. Combine 1 cup sugar, 1 cup flour, and 1 teaspoon baking powder in mixing bowl. Beat one large egg and stir into dry ingredients until crumbly. Spread over fruit, and then pour 1 cube of melted butter evenly over top. Bake at 375 degrees for 25 minutes. Eat warm with vanilla ice cream.

Pudding:

Homemade pudding is such a yummy dessert and taste much better than instant pudding from a box. I use a microwave recipe that's easy, and you don't have to worry about it sticking to the bottom of the pan when cooking. You can also use these recipes to make cream pies!

Vanilla Pudding: In a blender, measure out 3 cups of milk, 4 egg yolks, 1 1/8 cup sugar (1 cup plus 2 tablespoons), 4 1/2 tablespoons cornstarch, and 1/2 teaspoon salt. Blend well, pour into a microwaveable bowl, and cook for approximately 9 minutes until thickened, stirring every 2 minutes with a wire whisk. Add 3 tablespoons butter and 1 1/2 teaspoons vanilla, stirring until butter is melted. Cool to serving temperature and ENJOY!

Chocolate Pudding: Prepare the same as vanilla pudding, except use 1 1/2 cups sugar instead. When finished cooking, add 3 squares unsweetened chocolate, 3 tablespoons butter, and 1 1/2 teaspoons vanilla; stir until well mixed in. (Unsweetened chocolate can be made by mixing 3 tablespoons unsweetened cocoa with 1 tablespoon canola oil; this is the equivalent of 1 square.)

Banana Pudding: Prepare vanilla pudding and layer in serving dish with sliced bananas and vanilla wafers.

Rice Pudding: Prepare vanilla pudding, but before microwaving, add in 1 cup cooked rice. This is a much faster way to prepare rice pudding for a creamy evening dessert over the standard custard-style rice pudding.

Cookies:

My family loves cookies; the problem is, if the cookies get baked, they get eaten! I solved this problem by making large batches of cookie dough and either refrigerating it or making cookie dough balls and freezing them. This way, I can bake 1 pan of cookies—2 cookies for each family member, and we don't eat a whole batch in one evening. The following are my two favorite recipes.

Chocolate Chip Oatmeal: Beat 4 cubes (2 cups) butter, 2 cups brown sugar, and 2 cups white sugar together in large mixing bowl. Add in 4 eggs and 2 teaspoons vanilla, beat well. Then add 4 cups flour, 2 teaspoons baking soda, 2 teaspoons baking powder, and 1 teaspoon salt, mixing well. Measure 5 cups of oats and blend to a powder consistency. Add to cookie dough with 3 cups chocolate chips and mix well. Place teaspoonfuls on cookie sheet. Bake at 375 degrees for 9 minutes.

Peanut Butter Chocolate Chip: In large mixing bowl, beat together 4 cubes butter, 2 cups peanut butter, 2 cups brown sugar, and 2 cups white sugar. Beat in 4 large eggs and mix well. Then add 2 teaspoons baking soda, 1 teaspoon salt, and 4 cups flour. Mix well and add in 2-3 cups chocolate chips. Bake at 350 degrees for approximately 12 minutes. (Peanut Butter cookies are great soft and chewy or crispy brown with milk—ENJOY!)

Dough will keep in a covered container for up to 1 month in the refrigerator. Keeping dough made up will also give you a quick snack for unexpected guest and make your house smell delicious when they arrive. You will be prepared for last-minute plans, should they arise. This also allows you to bake just what your family needs, so cookies never go stale.

Ice Cream Sandwiches: Place 1 scoop of your favorite ice cream between 2 fresh cookies, press together and EAT! These are much better than ice cream sandwiches from the frozen food section at the grocery store, and your kids will think you're amazing!

Cakes:

One of my favorite homemade cakes is Angel Food cake. It can be easily decorated for any holiday or occasion. It also has a more dense consistency and much better flavor than those made from a box or purchased at the store bakery. It may take some practice but well worth the effort!

Angel Food Cake: 1 cup flour, 1 1/2 cups sugar, 1/4 teaspoon salt, 12 eggs, 1 1/4 teaspoon cream of tartar, and 1 1/4 teaspoon vanilla or almond extract. Sift together the flour, 3/4 cup sugar, and salt. In a separate bowl, beat egg whites with cream of tartar and extract until stiff peaks form (don't under beat). Add remaining sugar, 2 tablespoons at a time, beating well after each addition. Sift 1/4 cup flour mixture over beaten egg whites, and then fold in carefully; gradually fold in remaining flour by fourths. Spoon the cake mixture into a tube pan, and bake in preheated 375-degree oven for approximately 35-40 minutes or until cake looks dry and toasty brown on top. Cool by inverting the pan on a funnel or bottle. After completely cooling, remove from pan by running knife around all edges. Turn out onto a serving platter, and then frost with butter frosting (with sugar cookie recipe in Thanksgiving section) and decorate with colorful sprinkles.

Pies:

My daughter Briana prefers pies over cake. We have often made berry pie for her birthday rather than the traditional birthday cake. Because I get all the free blackberries I can pick from my parents, pies are a great and inexpensive solution to dessert.

To make one 9 inch pie, start by preparing a double pie crust using the recipe for crust in the Thanksgiving section. Then put 8 cups previously frozen blackberries in a pot, add 3/4 - 1 cup sugar, and bring to boil. Thicken to a good pie-filling consistency using a cornstarch and cold water blend...not too runny and not too thick. Pour berries into the crust, dot the top with butter, place the top crust on, crimp the edges, and make slits in the top. I like to sprinkle the top of the crust with sugar and cinnamon before baking. Bake at 400 degrees for approximately 45-50 minutes or until the filling is bubbling through the slits on top. You may need to cover with foil, should the crust get too brown before filling is done. Cool before serving.

Bread:

Our family loves homemade bread! I like this recipe because I can make any type of loaf or bun out of it that I need. Homemade bread also makes the best toast ever! Be patient, practice a lot, and you will be so glad you learned this art. Your family will love you for it!

Whole Wheat French Bread: Measure out 2 1/2 cups warm water in large measuring cup or bowl; add 2 tablespoons yeast and 3 tablespoons sugar. Stir and let stand until the sugar and yeast are dissolved while yeast rises. Meanwhile, in a large mixing bowl, combine 2 cups whole wheat flour (preferably fresh milled), 1 tablespoon salt, and 3 heaping tablespoons wheat gluten. Add 1/3 cup canola oil and yeast mixture to flour, mixing well for 3 minutes. Gradually add approximately 4 cups more flour, and then knead for 10-12 minutes. Let the dough rise to double, punch down, and shape into loaves. Make slits across the top (5 for big loaves, 3 for small loaves), brush with egg wash (1 beaten egg white with 1 tablespoon water) then let rise again. Bake at 375 degrees for 24 minutes.

Note: This recipe can be used for a variety of shaped loaves, dinner rolls, and hamburger buns. If making buns, flatten on pan before rising. Also, if you have access to it, adding 2 tablespoons of Dough Enhancer when mixing gives you a softer, lighter-textured bread.

Thanksgiving Dinner

I know many ladies who have been married for a number of years but have never cooked a Thanksgiving dinner. This could be for a number of reasons, including always spending the day at other homes or just simply out of fear, not knowing how to cook a big Thanksgiving turkey with all the trimmings. I trust this section will help you get organized and give you the knowledge you need to put on the best Thanksgiving dinner ever.

In 1863 Abraham Lincoln officially declared the last Thursday in November as a day of thanksgiving. This would be a day to remember our heritage and celebrate God's blessings and provisions, just as the Pilgrims did on the first Thanksgiving. I love to use garden vegetables and fruit whenever possible. Although I always prepare the traditional Thanksgiving meal, I also love to cook up wild game meat that God may have blessed us with during the year. At different times, we have prepared pheasant, deer, elk, and halibut caught in Alaska. This allows us the opportunity to share God's abundant provisions with others.

Organizing your time and knowing when or how early food items need prepared is a big part of cooking a successful Thanksgiving feast. As mentioned in the hospitality chapter, we traditionally prepare a Thanksgiving dinner the Wednesday evening before Thanksgiving Day inviting church family and friends who may not have anyone to share the day with. Although I always allow others to bring food items, I want everyone to come regardless of their ability to contribute and enjoy a fun time of celebration and relaxation. I must say, even though this is labor-intensive, it's my favorite meal to prepare each year.

My typical menu includes: turkey, dressing, mashed potatoes, sweet potatoes, corn, green beans, banana squash, green salad, fruit salad, Jell-O salad, macaroni salad, relish tray with olives, deli pickles, and deviled eggs, fresh cranberry relish, canned peaches, fresh whole wheat bread or rolls, applesauce bread, punch, pumpkin pie, blackberry pie, chocolate cream pie, coconut cream pie, cheese cake with blackberry topping, and leaf or pumpkin shaped sugar cookies.

You're probably thinking, "WOW that's a ton of food!" And you are so right, it is! I happen to believe if we can manage it, why not celebrate God's provisions in a BIG way with a BIG meal; 'cause GOD'S a BIG GOD!

I start three to five days in advance by placing the turkey in the refrigerator to thaw (how long depends on the size). Due to the fact that I prepare this dinner for Wednesday evening, I make all my desserts and breads on Tuesday. (Frosted sugar cookies actually soften overnight making them perfect to eat!) This frees up my oven for the turkey on Wednesday. However, I like to make the whipped cream or meringue for my cream pies the day I serve them. The day of the dinner, potatoes can be peeled, cut, placed in a pot and covered with water then set aside until 1 – 1 1/2 hours before dinner time. If using fresh sweet potatoes or yams, they can be cooked and placed in a pan with brown sugar on them ahead of time, ready to go in the oven. All veggies can go in pots early, waiting to be cooked. Salads can be made the morning of the dinner or started the day before while baking desserts. Fruit salad should be made up a little early, but make sure the bananas are added just before dinner so they don't turn brown. This may seem overwhelming but I assure you, it's possible and you will have a *blast* cooking. Invite someone over to help you, turn on some great music, and enjoy the *blessing* of preparing to bless others!

Note: I like having a few snacks out for guests to munch on while waiting for dinner. This might include mixed nuts and dried fruit, crackers, salami, cheese spread, and candies. This will ease the hunger pangs your guests experience while smelling the delicious dinner you are preparing!

Turkey: Select a turkey based on the size of group you are having. I typically cook a 25 pound turkey for approximately 40 people; I like a few leftovers for turkey sandwiches and quick meals over the weekend (since my husband and I do the day-after-Thanksgiving shopping blitz). An average-sized turkey would be about sixteen pounds. Be certain to thoroughly thaw turkey before cooking if you purchase it frozen. This could take up to 5 days in the refrigerator for a large bird.

To prepare after thawing, remove the giblets and neck from inside the turkey, and place them in a saucepan.

Cover with water, salt, and pepper then simmer until giblets are tender. (I use the broth for stuffing; giblets can be chopped and added to the dressing or gravy if desired. I place the neck in the pan and roast it with the turkey; it adds great flavor.) Meanwhile, rinse the turkey and make sure cavities are clean; salt inside of the cavity, stuff with dressing, then place on a rack inside a roasting pan. Pour a cube of melted butter over top of turkey, salt and pepper, cover with lid or heavy foil, and bake in the oven at 325 degrees. You need to plan approximately 20 minutes per pound of turkey. Using a baster, baste the turkey with drippings every hour the last 3 hours of baking. Also, remove lid or foil the last 20-30 minutes to brown the top. Cooking time will vary based on stuffing; a stuffed bird will take longer to cook. Determine doneness by using a meat thermometer, checking around the leg of the bird. (If you don't have a meat thermometer, I recommend investing in one.) Meat around bone takes longer to cook. The temperature should read between 160-170 degrees to be well done.

Dressing (Stuffing): You can make your own bread cubes, but purchasing a bag of cubes for stuffing is very inexpensive and will save you much time. Place bread cubes into a large bowl. Chop 1 small onion and 2 celery stalks; boil together until tender. When done, add to dry bread cubes. Then add 5 beaten eggs, 1-2 cans cream of mushroom soup, 2 teaspoons sage, 1 cup melted butter, 1 cup chicken broth (you can use the broth left from cooking giblets, adding some chicken base to it), garlic, salt, and pepper. Mix well together; the dressing should be moist but not too soggy. Adjust liquids as needed, and then stuff both cavities of the bird.

Mashed Potatoes: Cook the desired number of potatoes in a large pot until tender but not mushy. Beat with a hand mixer, adding in desired amounts of butter, sour cream, milk, salt, and pepper. Place in a serving dish and top with additional butter and pepper or paprika.

Gravy: Pour broth (drippings from the roasted turkey) into large pot and bring to a boil; blend 2 cups of milk with 1/3 cup flour and slowly stir into boiling broth. Using a wire whisk will help stir well and avoid clumps. Cook until thickened. Extra water, chicken base, or milk, and flour can be added as needed; salt and pepper to taste.

Candied Yams/Sweet Potatoes: Peel the sweet potatoes or yams and cut into large chunks; place in pan, cover with water, and cook until tender but not mushy. Drain water and place in baking dish. Cover top with brown sugar and pats of butter. Bake at 375 degrees until sugar and butter are melted. If desired, top with marshmallows and broil in the oven until toasty brown! Keep your eye on them so they won't get too hot and catch fire inside your oven.

Vegetables: I usually just add butter, salt, and pepper to my corn. For canned green beans, I like to add onion, garlic, mushrooms, bacon and/or bacon grease, butter, salt, and pepper. The best way to cook banana squash is to peel, cut in cubes, and cook until tender in a pan. Drain water then beat as you would for mashed potatoes except add brown sugar, butter, and salt.

Fresh Cranberry Relish: Put 1 pound of cranberries and 3 oranges (2 peeled) in a food grinder on a fine blade and grind. Add 1 1/2 cups sugar, one 20-ounce can crushed pineapple–drained, the juice of 2 lemons, and 1 cup coarsely chopped pecans or walnuts. Mix together then divide in half. Freeze half the mixture for later use. (I like to do one batch for Thanksgiving and freeze the other half to be used at Christmas. Dissolve a 3-ounce package of orange gelatin in 1 cup boiling water, and then pour over the cranberry mixture. Spoon into a pretty glass bowl, cover, and refrigerate for several hours before serving. (I like to use orange gelatin for Thanksgiving and raspberry gelatin for Christmas.)

Applesauce Bread: Dissolve 2 rounded tablespoons of yeast with 1/4 cup warm water. In a large mixing bowl, combine 1 cup warm applesauce, 1 cup softened butter, 2 beaten eggs, 1/4 cup sugar, and 1 teaspoon salt. Beat until well blended. Add 4 cups flour and 1 teaspoon grated lemon rind (optional). Beat until smooth, approximately 1 minute; dough will be soft and slightly sticky. Place in greased bowl, cover, and let stand at least 2 hours or overnight. (Dough will keep in refrigerator up to 4 days.)

Combine 1/2 cup sugar and 1 tablespoon cinnamon in a small bowl then set aside.

Divide dough into 4 equal pieces. Working with 2 pieces at a time, roll out the dough into 12x8-inch rectangles. Sprinkle each piece with 2 tablespoons of the sugar mixture, and then repeat with other 2 pieces of dough. Starting with the long side, roll each piece up from the long side. Place side by side and twist 2 rolls together; repeat with the other 2 rolls. Cover with a damp cloth, and place both braided loaves on a greased cookie sheet. Let the bread rise in a warm place until double in size then bake at 350 degrees for 25-30 minutes; remove from the oven and spread the top of each loaf with a glaze made from 2 heaping tablespoons applesauce, 2 tablespoons melted butter, and 1 cup powdered sugar. Beat until smooth.

Pies – Pie Crust: To make a double crust for a 9-inch pie, mix 2 cups flour and 3/4 teaspoon salt in a large bowl. Cut in 3/4 cup shortening into the flour mix until particles are very fine. Make sure and use a pastry cutter, as this gives you a more consistent texture. Using a fork, slowly stir in 4-5 tablespoons of cold water until dough sticks together but is not sticky. Press together in a ball and divide into 2 pieces—one for the bottom crust and one for the top. On a well floured table top, press and roll out 1 piece of dough until approximately 1/8-inch thick (or thinner). Fold the dough in half, and then gently lift the dough onto a pie pan, laying over the edges. Fill with pie filling, and then roll out the top crust. Make a design on the top before folding in half and placing over the top. Fold or roll the excess dough to form a thick edge all around the pie. Finally, using your thumb and fore-fingers, press the edges, making a crimping design.

For a single-crust pie, follow the directions above, except use 1 1/2 cups flour, 1/2 teaspoon salt, 2/3 cup shortening, and 3-4 tablespoons water. Using a fork, poke holes in crust then bake at 425 degrees for about 12 minutes or until golden brown.

Pumpkin Pie: I typically use the recipe for pumpkin pie filling from the Libby pumpkin can. Pour into an unbaked, single pie crust and follow the baking instructions on can.

Berry Pie: Start with 8 cups berries for a full pie. Place in large pot with 1 cup sugar. As berries begin to thaw, start heating on the stove. When berries come to a boil, thicken with cornstarch and water mix until you get a thick yet creamy filling. If it gets too thick, you won't have a creamy filling but if not thick enough it will be runny. This will take practice to get a good consistency, but keep working at it and you WILL perfect it! Pour filling into bottom crust, dot with 2-3 tablespoons butter, place on the top crust, then sprinkle with cinnamon and sugar. Fold foil up around the bottom of pie to catch any filling that bubbles over the top. Bake at 400 degrees for approximate 45 minutes or until filling is bubbling through the top slits.

Cream Pie: Use a baked, single pie crust. Make a batch of your favorite pudding and pour into the pie shell. You can top with cool whip, real whipped cream whipped with vanilla and powdered sugar, or make a meringue (out of leftover egg white).

Meringue: Beat 3-4 egg whites with 1 teaspoon of vanilla and 1 teaspoon cream of tartar until frothy. Gradually add 6 tablespoons of white, granulated sugar, and continue beating until the mixture looks very stiff and glossy and the sugar is dissolved. This will take approximately 5 minutes of beating on high speed with your mixer. It's hard to over beat, so DON'T UNDERBEAT!! Spread meringue on top of the pudding mix, and spread to the very edges of the pie crust, leaving no pudding exposed. I like to sprinkle with coconut if making a coconut cream pie or with chocolate chips if making a chocolate cream pie. You can make little peaks with a spatula by tapping meringue and quickly pulling up with spatula before adding any toppings. Bake at 400 degrees for approximately 7 minutes or until meringue is a nice golden brown, or at least the peaks are toasted. This will make your cream pies look professionally made, and you will be able to use the egg whites left over from the pudding so you have NO waste.

Bridgewaters' Favorite Cheese Cake: Make a graham cracker crumb crust by mixing 1 1/2 cups graham cracker crumbs, 3 tablespoons sugar, and 1/3 cup melted butter. Spread into a 13x9-inch pan and bake in oven at 300 degrees for 10 minutes. While baking, beat one 8-ounce package of cream cheese until smooth. Gradually beat in 1 can sweetened condensed milk until well blended; then beat in 1/2 cup lemon juice and 1 teaspoon vanilla. Pour over crumb crust and chill. Top with desired fruit pie filling or sprinkle the top with a few reserved graham cracker crumbs and serve. I usually use blackberries as a topping by placing 3 cups blackberries in a pan, add 1/2 cup sugar, and heat to boil. Then thicken with a little cornstarch and water mixture. Cool and spread on top. You can use any fruit or berries this way or purchase canned pie filling if preferred.

Sugar Cookies: Place 3/4 cup butter (use real butter), 2/3 cups sugar, 1/4 teaspoon salt, 2 egg yolks, 1 tablespoon milk, and 1 teaspoon vanilla in a large mixing bowl, and beat until smooth. Add 2 cups flour, and mix well until you have smooth dough. On a lightly floured counter top, roll out dough to approximately 1/4-inch thickness. Using cookie cutters, cut out cookies, placing them on an ungreased baking sheet. Bake in a preheated oven at 325 degrees for approximately 12 minutes or until edges are lightly brown. Cookies should be cool before frosting.

Frosting: Combine 4 cups powdered sugar, 1 beaten egg yolk, 1 1/2 teaspoons vanilla, 2 tablespoons light cream or milk, and 1/3 cup butter (softened to room temperature). Beat well until you have a smooth creamy frosting. You may need to adjust the milk a little bit if the frosting is too stiff. Also, food coloring can be added to get the desired color for decorative frosting. If needing multiple colors, divide frosting out in bowls based on the number of colors you need, and mix in the desired color.

Punch: In punch bowl, mix two 6-ounce cans frozen orange juice, 1 can frozen lemonade, and 6 cans of water. Place several scoops of orange or pineapple sherbet on top then pour approximately one liter of chilled ginger ale over the top. This makes the punch look foamy, festive, and beautiful; a nice, tart punch for the holidays!

Sparkling Cider: Mix your favorite juice half-and-half with ginger ale. This tastes like sparkling cider from the store for a fraction of the cost!

Lastly, please know that paper plates and utensils are *legal* on Thanksgiving, making clean up much easier and allowing more time for visiting or playing games with your guests.

All-in-all, have fun! This should be a day of remembering God's bountiful blessings! It might be a little stressful preparing a large meal that takes so much preparation, but keep your focus on God's wonderful provisions and the privilege of blessing others.

Christmas Open House

Christmas—that wonderful time of year when we give because God first gave to us! Having an open house is a great way to bless others and share with friends and family whom you might not otherwise see over the holidays. It is fun to share in a festive celebration, yummy snacks, and, most importantly, connecting with people who are part of your life.

Begin by planning a date that doesn't conflict with other major events such as holiday concerts in your community or church Christmas parties. December is always a busy month, so it can be challenging finding a date that works. One thought is to speak with your Pastor and offer to host a Christmas open house for him and his family. Sometimes Pastors are so busy, it's difficult for them to host events in their home, but if someone had the space and time, it could be a great blessing for them to be at an open house without hosting and doing all the work! They could just relax and connect with people while someone else is covering the details.

Here are some recipes and ideas for preparing an open house. You will want to pick and choose what works for you, add to the list, or simplify it. Keep in mind that it's so much more than the food people come for...it's connecting with others and meeting new friends! **Start planning and have a great party!**

When planning, make sure you have a good mix of sweets, salty snacks, and healthy items. (As I'm writing this, we just hosted another open house, and I remember what wonderful fun it is!) Following is a list of suggested food items you may want to prepare and serve.

Vegetable Tray: Make certain when selecting vegetables, you consider color and freshness. Presentation means a lot, and selecting multiple colors of veggies will make a beautiful display that your guests will love to munch on. I like baby carrots, broccoli, radishes, celery, sweet red-orange-yellow peppers, cherry or grape tomatoes, and cauliflower. Be certain to wash and trim the vegetables thoroughly, and then pile in sections on a serving platter. Serve with ranch dressing or dip.

Cracker & Cheese Tray: Arrange a variety of crackers on a platter then place a small dish in the center with a little cube of cream cheese and raspberry chipotle sauce poured over top. Chipotle and cream cheese makes a wonderful spread on the crackers.

Salami & Cheese: Slice a sausage stick and arrange it on a tray. Using 2-3 different types of cheese (my personal favorites are horseradish, colby-jack, pepper jack, and cheddar), slice and cut in squares then arrange around the salami. You may either use the crackers from the previous tray or arrange some here with the salami and cheese.

Cheese Ball: In a small mixing bowl, blend together one 8-ounce block of cream cheese, garlic, 1 small jar chopped pimentos, 2 chopped green onions, 1 tablespoon Worcestershire sauce, 1/2 teaspoon dry mustard, 1 cup shredded cheddar cheese, salt, and pepper. Beat well with mixer. Form into a ball, roll in nuts, and then chill. You may prefer to skip the nuts and spoon the mixture into a small dish, serving it soft for ease of spreading. Adjust all ingredients and seasonings to taste. Serve with crackers, cheese, and salami.

Tortilla Chips & Dip: Serve tortilla chips with any one or multiple dips. You can use salsa, bean dip, cheese dip, and guacamole with sour cream.

Chips & Dip: I may be a little traditional but I prefer Ruffles for dipping. Make a dip by combining 1 cup sour cream, 1 cup mayonnaise, 1 small ripe red tomato (diced); 1/2 pound crumbled crispy bacon pieces, salt, and pepper. If you like BLTs, you will love this dip! It's a must serve!

Mixed Nuts: In small serving bowl, mix cashews, pecans, almonds, dried cranberries, M & Ms, chocolate covered raisins, and chocolate covered almonds. Easy, healthy, and really yummy!

Bbq Little Smokies: Pour BBQ sauce over the desired amount of Little Smokies, and heat thoroughly on the stove or in a crock pot. These are always a big hit!

Cut Out Sugar Cookies: See Sugar Cookie and Frosting recipes in the Thanksgiving recipe section. I love making a double batch of these, decorating them with colorful frosting and sprinkles then displaying trays in different rooms, including living, dining, and family rooms. This is a fun, yummy way to decorate for Christmas and clean up is easy...you just eat the décor!

Macaroons: Beat 3 eggs whites until stiff; add an 8-ounce package of coconut and 1 cup sugar. Mix well until smooth, no lumps. Drop by rounded teaspoon full onto a brown paper bag; place on top of a cookie sheet, and bake at 325 degrees for approximately 30 minutes. Cool and remove by wetting the back of the bag. Yields approximately 3 dozen cookies.

Chow Mein Cookie: Mix 1 can Chow Mein noodles with 12 ounces of butterscotch chips and 6 ounces of chocolate chips, melted together. Drop by teaspoonful onto wax paper, allowing cooling and getting firm.

Russian Teacakes: Thoroughly mix 1 pound butter (softened at room temperature), 1 cup powdered sugar, 2 teaspoons vanilla, 4 cups flour, 1/2 teaspoon salt, and 1 1/2 cups chopped pecans. Form dough into 1-inch balls, place on ungreased cookie sheets, and bake at 400 degrees for 8 minutes or until lightly browned. Roll into powdered sugar while hot. Cool completely then roll again in powdered sugar.

Peanut Butter Balls: In mixing bowl, place 1 1/2 cups graham cracker crumbs, 1/2 cup finely chopped pecans, 1 cup coconut, 12 ounce jar (or 1 1/2 cups) crunchy peanut butter, 3 1/2 cups powdered sugar, and 1 tablespoon vanilla. Pour 1 cup melted butter over the top and mix thoroughly. Form into walnut-sized balls, and chill in the refrigerator for at least 2 hours. Dip in melted chocolate (8 ounces chocolate chips and 1 tablespoon shortening), and allow the balls to firm on wax paper.

Peanut Brittle: Measure out 1 1/2 tablespoons butter, 1 1/2 teaspoons vanilla, and 2 teaspoons soda; set aside. In a heavy 3-quart saucepan, combine 1 cup light corn syrup, 2 cups sugar, and 1/2 cup water. Cook to very-soft ball stage (230 degrees at sea level), stirring occasionally. Add 1 pound of raw Spanish peanuts and cook, stirring occasionally to crack stage (301 degrees). Leave on the stove with the heat turned off, and stir in butter and vanilla. Last of all, stir in the baking soda, and work quickly as candy will foam up. Immediately pour the candy onto a buttered 17x 11 inch roasting pan and spread to the edges. Let the candy cool, and then break into pieces. This is a wonderful and traditional holiday candy.

Fabulous Fudge: In a large bowl mix 3 cups chopped nuts, 18 ounces (or 3 cups) chocolate chips (or any other flavor you like), 1/2 pound (2 cubes) butter, 6 cups mini marshmallows, 1/2 teaspoon salt, and 2 teaspoons vanilla. In a large pot, bring to boil one 12-ounce can evaporated milk and 4 1/2 cups sugar; simmer or boil lightly for 10 minutes, stirring constantly. Pour the milk mixture over the other ingredients, and stir well until all ingredients are melted and blended together. Pour into a buttered sheet pan to cool. Varieties of fudge can be made by using other flavored chips or mixing flavors into "white" fudge. We made huckleberry fudge this past Christmas by swirling thawed huckleberries into the mixture.

Beverages: Coffee, hot tea, sodas, or punch made with orange juice, cranberry juice, raspberry/orange sherbet and ginger ale.

Certainly, you don't have to serve everything here, but this will give you some suggestions. Also, don't feel bad if you have to purchase some quick-fix items from the store such as breaded shrimp, tacquitos, or egg rolls. You can also use tortillas to make little sandwich roll-ups with thinly sliced meat and cheese. The options are limitless; just remember to have fun. It's easy to work so hard that you're too tired to enjoy the evening. The guests you invite are what this celebration is all about so relax and ENJOY!

I trust this section is a handy guide to help you launch into easy meal planning and preparation, providing wonderful meals at a fraction of the cost it takes to eat out or purchase prepared and pre-packaged items from the store. As mentioned in the chapter on cooking, don't be afraid of *messing up* a recipe; just eat what you can salvage, feed the rest to the dog, and if all else fails, toss it and start over. Be diligent to the task and you will have success! You will eat healthier, heartier, and save money all at the same time. So, roll up your sleeves, don that apron, and **START COOKIN'**!

Tag from Tim, a husband's perspective:

If you will use this guide, your family will rise up with wonderful words of constant praise. There will be dancing in the streets, ticker tape parades, and a special chair just for you in the church. Okay, probably not. However, your family will be grateful, and your guests will enjoy the blessings received by your hands. So go ahead and get started adding a large dose of love to every recipe.

Thoughts from the Bridgewater Kids

At a ladies' retreat in Challis, Idaho, last year, I was approached by guest speaker, Pastor Dottie Schmitt, who spoke this prophetic word of knowledge to me: "I see a book in you." Explaining to Pastor Dottie that I had just started the early processes of laying out a book, she encouraged me to allow my children to contribute something. After speaking to them, my kids were all in agreement. The only direction I gave them in regards to writing was to think about what it was like growing up in our home. What you read here is what they wrote and gave me (with limited editing). I understood that this assignment would bring a deeper level of transparency to our family. You will see that we've had ups and downs; not perfection, but all in all, a *real* family, which I believe everyone can relate to in one way or another. I trust you enjoy reading "Thoughts from the Bridgewater Kids."

Benjamin (Ben), Age 22:

We have all run into those people who claim they are *busier than thou* and gloat to the presence of impending stress for the innumerable amount of appointments that are supposedly piling on top of each other in their calendar thus proclaiming: "I am so busy I just don't know what to do." So the implied response expected from this complainer who is digging and prodding for you to ask is, "Why are you so busy?" We all know however, that by asking the question, we are going to get an exhaustingly exaggerated list which we really don't care to hear about in the first place only to find they aren't as busy as they claim and bring unneeded stress into their lives by procrastinating on the small details of normal everyday life. It has been said if you have a much needed task to be accomplished, give it to the one who has the most on their plate, a busy person.

Growing up in a family of eight kids brings an obvious yet somewhat unimaginable amount of busyness and sheer stress into the family picture. When someone says they are busy I can't help but smile a little on the inside and think, *You don't know busy until you meet the mother of eight kids and a husband who is just as dependent upon and sometimes more in need of attention.* Now I'm not necessarily saying that my father is incapable of sufficiently managing a house full of people, and I'm not saying there is a role play deficiency because my father is definitely the head of our home and models closely the biblical view of marriage on the home front. What I am saying is that my mother is extremely busy but is not one of those who groans to bring attention, rather she is happy at the work that bombards her when her alarm goes off at 5:30 a.m.

Time, Money, and Intimacy are three of the most vital parts of a marriage. When arguments and fights arise in the home, the root of the problem often involves these issues. When considering this, it would make sense that fights were a normal part of everyday life for us kids growing up as we unintentionally took internal notes, evaluating the relationship between our parents, but this was not the case.

A healthy income and the conveniences that wealth can supply were never a part of our home. Our family was sustained from one income and many prayers. My dad, being a minister of a small body of believers, brings in a minimal amount of money. Literally our family often ate the very last portions of food the days leading up to payday and even rationed the remaining supplies that we might make it and be sustained till payday. This gave us no room for unforeseen expenses, like the car breaking down or home repairs. Distress leading to arguments in a marriage because of the lack of money would be likely in this scenario.

To pastor a small congregation is very time-consuming and often more involved than a mega-church because the responsibilities remain the same despite the size of a church. The only difference is the number of clergy and congregants involved to handle the work load. Working seven days a week at sixty to seventy hours per week became a normal routine for my dad as he worked hard in the area of ministry he felt called. People often say, "You're lucky your dad is a pastor. He only has to work one or two days a week." I can only say I wish that were true. So ultimately in my parent's marriage there was little time and money; but what about intimacy? Obviously they made good in this area resulting in eight of us kids, but I have to say that even in their intimacy they must have had a hard time making this work; when they sent everyone to bed it would often be a constant struggle with one of the kids needing something that just couldn't wait. First hand I know that bed time was often interrupted with a small knock at the bedroom door and a little voice saying I'm thirsty, or I can't sleep, etc.

Three areas which play a vital role in a successful marriage are being continually compromised for fairly obvious reasons given the circumstances. This being said I can honestly say that my parents rarely or never fight. Understandably there would be room for a fight here or there about something, anything due to the immeasurable amounts of stress. However, even as extraordinarily uncommon as this might be and sound, this is the truth coming from the oldest; having been around them as a couple longer than anyone else, again I tell you that fighting at least in front of a young, innocent audience was never seen or accepted in my parents relationship. I can honestly say that I have never, to my knowledge, witnessed them in a fight in my twenty-two plus years of life and am saddened that this is not the norm for most families. I have talked to friends and groups about family relationships that had been everything but calm. They say to me, "You are fortunate to have such amazing parents as you do," and I nod to agree and could only say I wished that were the case for them. You see they came from an environment where divorce was not only feared as an option, but an unfortunate future reality as the word divorce was thrown around flippantly. I am deeply saddened that this is happening in families all around me. I could not imagine or bear the thought of that being a possibility in my family. Divorce was not a part of their vocabulary nor did the thought even glance across their mind for a minute, and for this I am so grateful.

My parents have always done their best to raise the family in the best way they possibly could with the help of God, prayer, and biblical influence. This by no means exempts them from error. I believe they would tell you the same, and that if they could do it again they might even change some things. In the end I can honestly say I am grateful and thank God that he provided me with parents who strive to be Christ-like in all decisions they make. I write this with the hope it might impact husbands and wives in their response to one another for the benefit of their own emotional distress and vowed relationship to one another, as well as the innocent bystanders known as their children. I don't think anyone should ever stop learning how to communicate and relate to others in hopes to better understand and respond when placed in a position of deciding whether to fight or unite for the good of the entire family.

Benjamin, graduate from Southwestern Assemblies of God University with a degree in Pastoral Ministry. He is currently serving on church staff as Associate/Youth Pastor.

Jesse, Age 20:

When I was six years old my dad took my brother and me to a music store. When we went inside, the store clerk asked if there was anything he could help us find, and my dad told him he wanted to look at some smaller sized guitars. Immediately, my heart started beating faster as we walked into a dimly lit room that just so happened to have two miniature electric guitars, a blue one and a black one. The black one instantly caught my eye, and for the rest of the day I couldn't stop thinking about how much I wanted that amazing instrument. Unfortunately, we left that day without the guitar. A few months later, at Christmas time, I received a gift from my parents that I never would have asked for, a strange looking cable thing. With an awkward look on my face, I turned to my parents to say thanks when it clicked; this was a guitar cable for my new miniature jet-black electric guitar.

Since that day my interest in music increased, but it wasn't until I was 14 that my passion for music really starting growing as my parents encouraged me to learn the drums and bought me a new guitar for my birthday when I was 15. My love for music continued to grow as I played drums and guitar on our church worship team and went to a church camp where I felt called to the ministry of worship and music. After graduating from high school and working for two years, I knew I wanted to go to a college where the main focus was on the Bible and music. One day, I was telling a friend about my dream college and she happened to know of a school in Australia that seemed to fit my desires. After doing some research, I decided that this was the place for me but didn't think my parents would ever agree to me moving halfway around the world and going to a college that was way more than I could afford. Despite what I imagined my parents saying, I told them anyway and was surprised by their response. They were extremely supportive and encouraged me to follow my dreams and calling and told me that this school sounded like the perfect college for me; and that even though it was going to cost a lot of money, they knew that if it was where God wanted me then He would make a way. After six months of planning and preparation, I was off to the college of my dreams. I know it would have never happened without the support of my mom, dad, and of course, God. I like to think it all started with that little black guitar and parents who could dream right along with me and understand my passions.

Jesse, completed 2 year program at Hillsong Leadership College in Sydney Australia and currently serving on church staff as Music/Creative Arts Pastor.

Josiah (Joey), Age 19:

Growing up in a large family, I have experienced a whole different kind of "crazy." Living with seven siblings teaches you so much about every day values. Whether it's working as a team, learning to save your money, or being home on time for dinner, all play an important role in the Bridgewater home. It was critical that we all worked together. I know this is true of most families, but when you don't unify in a large family, there are more people affected. I am very appreciative that my parents taught us the importance of everyone pitching in to help at such a young age. We were required to do our daily chores, but received no allowance in return. Another valuable lesson my parents taught us from a young age is to save our money. Because we received no allowance, it was up to us to find small jobs around the neighborhood. I began working for an elderly neighbor lady at the young age of six. It was at that time I not only learned good work ethics, but also money management skills. I believe if you begin teaching these important lessons to children at a young age it will stick with them throughout their life. Lastly, an important thing I learned growing up in my family was to be on time for dinner. If we showed up late, food was usually all gone by the time we got home. The only exception to this rule was when my mom dished up plates for those who were working or engaged in other important activities. I am so thankful for this because there were many nights I would come home from a late night at work and was able to heat up my dinner in the microwave. This saved me from going hungry, having to prepare my own meal, or eating fast food; UGH! Dinner from scratch was so much better! Thanks Mom for thinking of me!

Josiah, Distance Ed student at Southwestern Assemblies of God University pursuing a Children's Ministry/Writing degree and currently serving on church staff as Children's and Missions' Pastor

Briana (Bri), Age 16:

Blonde jokes; everyone hears them, and everyone has one to tell. But in my family I am the one they get told about, like I am somehow the *dumb blonde*! Well I'm here to tell you that I'm not that dumb blonde, but I do tend to talk a lot. I am what some may call the lively one of the group. And for me, my life is a little different than most, for obvious reasons of course. I have grown up in a rather large family which consists of a mom, a dad, and seven brothers, yes ... seven. And yes ... I am the only girl! Throughout my life I have grown up with what you could call protection by older brothers that like to constantly run the boys off. But I have been blessed with the opportunity to be able to protect my younger siblings as well. Having seven brothers has made me the tough girl at school, and has really taught me life skills, such as knowing how to protect myself against harm. The privilege to having as many siblings as I do definitely has its ups and its downs.

Ups:

Always tons of laughter among the family.
Someone to put a smile on my face.
Knowing how to protect myself along with others.
Learning outstanding household skills such as: knowing how to cook, clean, baby sit, obey, understand, listen, love one another, and many more.

Downs:

What can I say? There's never enough food around the house.

Disagreements between all siblings at the same time.

Not enough privacy for someone of my age, being the only girl.

Breaking up fights between younger siblings over the Xbox 360 that my dear friend Chrissie so kindly gave to them for Christmas; thanks Chrissie!!

Nap times are rare! (This is probably the worst part of it and I think my parents agree.)

Now don't get me wrong; I love my family, although there may be a few mishaps along this long, adventurous road, I wouldn't trade them for the world.

My family may not look like or be "The American Dream Family" but as a whole we know how to work through our differences to make us stronger. My family is unlike most families out there and that isn't just because of how huge it is; but because of the uniqueness that comes out of it. My parents have unconditional love for each other, my brothers and me. For the most part we get along, and although we may not be the richest family on this incredible planet, we have each other and in my heart I truly believe that the bond of love is far stronger than any bond that riches may bring. Because of the family I have been raised in with my father being a pastor, my standards have been raised on how I should walk, talk, dress, behave, and much more that comes along with it. I also want everyone to know that just because I am a pastor's kid, doesn't mean I'm perfect; in fact no one is perfect! (Ponder that for a moment☺.) I have made mistakes in life, that at the moment I want so badly to take back, but in the long run have served to make me stronger. I have taken my wrong doings and made them a tool for my own life, to learn from.

My parents have taught me a lot in my lifetime and I think the biggest thing is to simply listen. Now you may be thinking, "Listening isn't so hard", but if you break it down, it's harder than you think. If there was one thing I could change about all these years I have lived, it would be to simply learn to listen better; and when I say listen, I mean do what your parents ask of you, listen to the advice they so firmly pound into your brain like it's some sort of food for your mind. As a teenager myself, I am speaking to all teens out there. Really listen! Don't take the advice your mother and father give you and throw it out the window; because in all reality, you could make decisions you wished you never made if you don't listen. My parents have raised my siblings and me well. My mom makes home cooked meals nearly seven days a week (That's nearly every day of her life!) and not only that she cleans, does laundry, helps out with homework, helps my father, and somehow finds time to look for new jackets in the latest magazines; and she also sends dear friends heartwarming messages on Facebook. But that's beside the point. You see, she understands and is willing to help settle a situation/conflict that may be happening at that moment. Whereas my father does all that and so much more and on top of all that, can raise eight children. So I guess you could say I have lived a pretty good life. Life has its bumps and rough patches that may bring you down, but the hard times in life are the times that are there only given to make us stronger and wiser. I believe the hardest times in my life have been some of the best times in life simply because they taught me lessons and made me value everything in my life twice as much, making me a better person. Life is an adventure; take it and make the most of it. Press forward into new and better things that are worth living for. Don't stress over the little things, but find joy in them. Never give up on who you are, or who you want to become.

Briana, High School Junior with goals for college degree in secondary education and ministry.

Isaac, Age 15:

I think that growing up in a big family has been outrageous. There is so much to be done in order to keep everyone on the same page. One thing we need to do is to clean up after ourselves. When you have ten people beneath one roof it can get really cruddy around the house extremely fast. So if we all do our own part in cleaning the house it will take more pressure off of my parents and they can focus on more important things like providing for the family.

My parents have taught me many lifelong lessons. One lesson my parents taught me was to never give up and wow that is the most important rule of all times in my opinion. Why do I think this? Well because without learning this rule I would never have achieved so many things and some of the things still to come. Learning this lesson has helped me so much during the sports I play. I have played football for going on seven years now. I have also wrestled for a couple years of my life. During these sports I had many times where I felt like skipping practice. I did not skip even though I wanted to and when it all came down to it I am so happy that I didn't because then I would have felt like I let down the team. Also one year in football I tore a back muscle in a game. Even though I tore my muscle and knew that I would not play much more, if any, for the rest of the year, I still went to the practices and watched as my team practiced. Also another time that this lesson came in handy was when I first started my lawn business. My first year doing this job I had to hook up a trailer on the back of my bike and then put all of my lawn mowing equipment on it which included my lawn mower and weed eater. I had to ride about a mile for one of my jobs and then of course after I was done I had to ride back. There were a couple times that I felt like giving up. I never did give up and it has paid off so far. One more story that I want to tell is that I used to struggle a lot in school. When I was in the sixth grade I had the reading level of a second grader. Through this time I just hated school and never wanted to try. Now that I am in the ninth grade I have a reading level of a ninth grader. This just goes to show that my parents did a marvelous job of teaching me this lesson to never give up! Isaac, High School Freshman with future goals in ministry and working with children.

Andrew (Andy), Age 12:

Having a family the size that I do is always fun and crazy at the same time! It's fun to go fishing and even when some of my brothers are gone, there is still someone left to go fishing with. The crazy part is that things always come up or happen just when we are getting ready to go somewhere. We have to learn to be really flexible. I like growing up in a big family!

Andrew, 7th grade student and still seeking God for future direction in ministry.

Aaron, Age 10:

Growing up with six brothers and one sister is hard sometimes, especially when they all like to tell you what to do. My little brother and I really wanted to go to public school so my mom let us. This has been a whole new experience for me. I got to meet a lot of new friends and some I already played football with. I get to play basketball with them too. In school, I had the opportunity to play in a concert. My teacher is really nice but you don't want to be around him if he gets mad. My principle is really nice too! I enjoy meeting and getting to know more people and new friends. I'm glad my dad and mom let me go to school.

Aaron, 5th grade, plays football and loves Jesus.

Christopher, Age 8:

I think my mom is cool because she cooks good food like steak. Also she takes me to the store when I need new clothes. When we go on bike rides, I always stay next to her. She takes care of me when I am sick. I also think my mom is cool because she lets me go to my friend's house on Sundays after church. Mom always gives me hugs!

Christopher, 2nd grade, plays backyard football and loves Jesus a whole bunch too!

Tag from Tim, a husband's perspective:

I trust you can understand we are a real family pursuing God with everything that is in us. It is true, we don't always hit the mark, but we press forward keeping our eyes on the prize. I can honestly say with all of our shortcomings and busyness, I wouldn't trade my life, my wife, or family for anyone or anything. God has truly blessed me beyond measure, and I am confident if you follow God, He will bless you too as you endeavor to live out His Word from day to day. In everything you do, do it as unto the Lord.

Conclusion

As women, we live in such a fast-paced, crazy world which can lead to feelings of unsettledness, chaos, and a lack of peace. "Domestic Diva" is meant to give you a sense of control over the domestic affairs of your home, bringing peace in the midst of chaos. It should encourage you to see yourself as a *Domestic Diva*, which by definition is a "glamorous and successful female performer and personality, caring for the affairs of the home; exuding much *domesticity,* showing affection for her children, home, and all the material components involved in such."

The Proverbs 31 woman excelled in demonstrating what it meant to be a *Domestic Diva* and so can you as a 21st century woman. You have likely seen the movies where a woman messes up her hair, throws a little flour on the front of her apron, and puts on an exhausted demeanor when her husband walks in the door, all the while she's baking a pre-packaged meal in the oven; who's fooled by this picture? I challenge you to prepare a *real* meal from scratch, don a cute pair of jeans or skirt with your high heels and apron, fix your hair, put on your favorite perfume, be spunky, have fun, and when your hubby walks in the door after work, trust me, he will be impressed!

Will you ever get tired? Oh yeah, exhausted to be exact! Take time to rest then push through the weariness and be intentional about having joy in your home as you work to be the best *Domestic Diva* ever! And yes, as God's Word proclaims, "The joy of the Lord IS your strength!"

I challenge you today to be who you were intentionally created to be—a **Domestic Diva,** glamorous and successful in personality and performance in the home; one that loves and shows affection to her children and husband. Just think of the rewards awaiting you: happy, healthy children who will rise up and bless you; a husband who will openly compliment you before others; and God who is honored because you have done everything you can to be a help meet, homemaker, and **Domestic Diva**, just as He called you to be!

Finally my sisters, know that God's ways are always the best. Following God's call and plan for your life will result in peace and satisfaction. I want to leave you with a few scriptures to encourage you to keep pressing on:

Romans 11:29: "For the gifts and the calling of God are irrevocable." Know that difficult days will come but during those times, you can look back to the calling and gifts God has equipped you with for the work ahead, assured that you *are* where God wants you to be!

Hebrews 6:10: "For God is not unjust to forget your work and labor of love which you have shown toward His name in that you have ministered to the saints, and do minister." God will never forget your hard work as you labor diligently and tirelessly in your call to the precious family He blessed you with.

Psalm 90:17: "And let the beauty of the Lord our God be upon us and establish the work of our hands for us; Yes, establish the work of our hands." Put on the beauty of the Lord that He may establish all your works which He called you to. I assure you, beauty and joy will overflow when you minister to your family.

I Corinthians 15:58: "With all this going for us, my dear, dear friends, stand your ground and don't hold

back. Throw yourselves into the work of the Master, confident that nothing you do for Him is a waste of time or effort." (The Message Bible) Know that everything you do to fulfill your call to your home and family will be as unto God, none of it is a waste of time no matter how mundane or seemingly useless. Throw yourself into the work of pursuing your title of "Domestic Diva."

Work diligently, serve tirelessly, and be as you were intentionally created to be, a real *DOMESTIC DIVA*!!